Also by Tom Cox

21st-Century Yokel
Close Encounters of the Furred Kind
The Good, The Bad and The Furry
Talk to the Tail
Under the Paw
Bring Me the Head of Sergio Garcia
Nice Jumper

Help the Witch

TOM COX

Unbound

This edition first published in 2018

Unbound
6th Floor Mutual House, 70 Conduit Street, London W1S 2GF

www.unbound.com

Text design by PDQ

A CIP record for this book is available from the British Library

ISBN 978-1-78352-669-7 (trade hbk)
ISBN 978-1-78352-671-0 (ebook)
ISBN 978-1-78352-670-3 (limited edition)

Printed and bound by CPI Group (UK) Ltd, Croydon, CR0 4YY

'The house . . . was old enough and large enough – and had seen enough dark acts – to support a ghost'

John Cheever, *The Wapshot Chronicle*

CONTENTS

Help the Witch	3
Listings	59
Speed Awareness	73
Nine Tiny Stories About Houses	85
The Pool	103
Robot	125
Just Good Friends	131
Folk Tales of the Twenty-Third Century	181
Seance	209
An Oral History of Margaret and the Village by Matthew and Five Others	221

HELP THE WITCH

6 DECEMBER

I have arrived! It feels like more of an achievement than I ever imagined it could. The snow started a little south of Northampton and became heavier all the way from there. A sensible person might have stopped long before that and checked into a hotel, but I am not a sensible person: I think, if there is one thing that this entire endeavour proves, it is that. I don't know how I got up to the top of the mountain (I have checked the altitude in feet, and it does technically qualify as a mountain). The two routes I'd used before were totally non-navigable in a normal car but somehow the more gentle incline to the east worked out: the snow had not quite settled as thickly there. It still took forty minutes of violently revving in first gear and hanging on to the steering wheel for dear life, though. In the end I had to reverse into the track, then let the car spin back round. If aliens gazed down from above at the patterns I left in the snow, they might mistake it for a violent, impulsive form of art. But I am here. We are here. Nibbler, A Good Size Cat, and me. Just the three of us, an airbed, a sleeping bag, a kettle and a rucksack. The house feels bigger than I remember, and cold. There's a lot of space in the top of the rooms, room for another room, really, in each. I find myself looking up into the space a lot. I'm exhausted, so I won't write more. I fear I might gibber if I do.

7 DECEMBER

My hands are covered in burns. I've been running on pure adrenaline for a fortnight, and because of that I never took the time to look at the state of them until this morning, when I was washing them. This might suggest that I had not washed them for several days. I had; I just hadn't noticed that I had hands. Before I left the cottage in Sussex I lit a giant bonfire, which burned for three days. You can take a dramatic angle on this, but I don't see it that way. It is true that I did burn some old letters from Chloe, but I also burned far more old phone bills, chequebooks and receipts. I was drawing a line, I suppose, but the themes of the line were largely relocation and confidential waste.

The burns on my hands are not battle scars, they're namby-pamby, middle-class injuries. But Niall, one of the two removal men, who I sense is not middle class, did glance at the red blisters on my right wrist, and ask if I was OK. He and his colleague, Dan, performed a minor act of heroism to even get the van halfway down the track today. With their time constraints I had to muck in and help with the carrying. My speed and capacity to take weight amazed me, made me re-appreciate those stories you hear about mothers who somehow find the strength to lift entire cars off their children. I'm six foot four but built like a bunch of long, sellotaped-together twigs, so adrenaline is the only explanation for what I've achieved in physical terms over the last few days. I have an equal lack of doubt that at some point I'm going to crash, but that point is yet to arrive. All the furniture and boxes are in now, although snow has drenched most of it.

No doubt Niall and Dan don't blink an eyelid at any of this – they've moved all sorts of people to all sorts of places in all sorts of weather – but I did notice them give me a certain kind of look a few times. The look was perhaps at its most noticeable when they said goodbye and wished me the best in my new home. If you drew the look, it might resemble some kind of wilting, half question mark. Was it pity? Bewilderment? A bit of both? I imagine they saw the cottage in Sussex as a very gentle, safe place and wondered why anyone would abandon it for here. I can see why they might think that, but it is all more complex than that and I am sure I've done the right thing. Maybe they were just worried about how tired I looked.

Last night, again, I failed to sleep in the part of the night traditionally designated for sleep. After conking out on top of the bedcovers at eight, I awoke to the sound of the blizzard pelting the thick walls of the house and either Nibbler or A Good Size Cat making a mournful wibbling noise, probably A Good Size Cat. Chloe named him A Good Size Cat because we'd yet to come up with the right name and, when we took him in for neutering, our vet called him 'a good size cat'. After that, Chloe kept saying, 'Look at this good size cat,' or, 'Where is the good size cat?' and it kind of stuck. He's the bigger of the two, as you might think with that name, but he is prone to night terrors. I got up and located them both, squatting nervously on a window ledge, looking out into a night of answerless black, but was surprised to find that the mournful wibbling sound continued, and was coming from neither of their mouths.

The house is joined, being half of a mid-Victorian farmhouse, but next door is currently empty: has been for God knows how long. My nearest neighbour is my landlord. After about half a mile the track divides, with my building on one side and his on the other, about 700 yards further down into the valley where the trees begin to close in. He is a petless person, a man I do not take for an animal lover. After that, there's not another house until you reach the next farmhouse, which – though their land abuts my landlord's – is a full mile away. Soon after this the village gradually begins to materialise in the form of a row of grey pebbledash semis. Having written off 'neighbour's pet' as an explanation, I did admittedly think 'ghost cat', but I don't believe in ghosts and I am tired. The most likely explanation is rats.

I sat on the top stair for a couple of hours, while Nibbler and A Good Size Cat paced anxiously and listened as the noise moved around the walls and ceilings. No doubt I could have used the time more constructively by being asleep, but I also think upon moving to a new house that it's useful to take some time to get accustomed to all the unfamiliar sounds the place makes, and there are plenty here: the 'whuooop-whuooop' of the wind passing through the cooker's extractor, the eerie tinkle of the thermostat as it resets, the snow pelting the walls, the branch of an overgrown willow thwacking the wall of what will soon be my study, the windy creak of a corrugated door of a barn, and the rats, if that's what they are. I made myself a Cup-a-Soup, then read a few chapters of a book about the history of the area, purchased in a charity shop after my first viewing of the house. I spent the final few hours before the slow winter dawn sitting up in bed thinking about the people who built the house for weather like this, building the house in weather like this.

8 DECEMBER

When I first came to see the house, at the beginning of last month, a smattering of leaves still clung to the trees. It was the final mild day of autumn and I broke into a sweat as I climbed to the top of the gritstone edge that acts as a natural architrave for the opposite valley wall. I stripped down to my T-shirt and skipped over stones and decided that the north of our country was no different from the south, besides the fact that it was bigger, more beautiful, and more real. Why would anybody in their right mind not want to live here? But today as I walked to the top of the track, I had difficulty accessing my mental picture of that day; it was impossible to imagine that any of the trees had ever been in leaf. I noticed the bare double sycamore that announced the mouth of the track, and realised more than before how it appeared to resemble a giant living scarecrow with enormous branch hands reaching up to the sky, about to wreak raging havoc upon an unjust universe.

Over on the adjacent side of the valley the edge was smoked in fog – fog that was all threat, all future, fog that could never be mistaken for mist, with all mist's nostalgia – and the only other person I spotted was the tenant farmer, laying traps for moles. He called hello to me and I wandered over. He introduced himself as Peter Winfield. He only works here, and lives down in the village. I put him at about my age, and he has a boyishness about him, but his face also speaks of the life he lives: it's a face full of weather, very little of it over 6° Celsius.

'So what you do think of him?' he said.

'Who?' I said.

'Him over there. Old Conkers. T'landlord.'

'I don't really know, yet. He seems OK. He doesn't smile much. I expected the house to be a bit cleaner.'

'Tight-fisted, he is. I'd watch him if I were you. He owns all of this but he never even looks at it. Stays inside the house all the time.'

The snow stopped mid-morning, but there's no thaw in evidence and zero chance of getting out in the car. Probably won't be for several days. I stocked up on food before I left Sussex and have plenty of tins dating from quite some time ago – many purchased in the Chloe Era by Chloe – but already I am making mental calculations about how long what I have got will last. Can a two-years-out-of-date can of kidney beans be reasonably counted as a meal? I walked down a narrow ravine into the village, looking for sustenance. Beneath my feet, the limestone path felt like a wet tablecloth being pulled from beneath me. The pub was closed, but in the tea room I was served a large plate of beans, scrambled egg, some bread, and half a tomato. I get the impression vegetarian meals will not be easy to come by here. I told the lady in the tea room I had just moved in up the hill. 'Oh, you should have said!' she replied. 'Residents get thirty per cent discount.'

Between the gritstone cottages the streets were corridors of silence, like everyone had shut themselves indoors to hide from a notorious wolf, and when a van door slammed up the road it sounded like an event. The churchyard is vast and all around the village – in fields, in spinneys and copses, even in gardens – are additional graves, marked and unmarked. When the Great Plague arrived here in the 1660s, the residents chose to seal themselves in, in an attempt to not spread it to other villages nearby. The most desolate sight of all is about half a mile outside the west end of the village where, in a field beneath a landslip, directly under an old oak, seven graves stand alone, enclosed by a wall. It was here that, according to legend, Winifred Cowlishaw – without assistance, in the space of one week – buried her six children and her husband, all of whom had succumbed to the virus. I do not think I have seen a more bleak spot in the whole of this country.

Back at home this evening, I listened to the rats again. I am not sure it's actually rats. It's not a collective or various sound: it's focused, has a persona and a certain autonomy as it goes about its business in the walls and, sometimes, apparently, in that big pocket of empty air at the top of the rooms, where there is space for another room. Also, there's no scurrying to go with it. Nibbler and A Good Size Cat seem spooked, constantly turning around abruptly at invisible frights. But isn't that just cats all over, all the time? Outside, the dark is very dark. But in the day, the whiteness is very dark too, sometimes even darker.

10 DECEMBER

The energy crash is finally happening. Last night, I saw the pepper mill move eight inches, all of its own volition. I could barely eat the mushroom risotto I made for myself without falling face first into it. Afterwards, I yanked my top half into bed, my legs following several yards afterwards, and heard the ghost cat make a new noise, much more questioning in tone. All this means, of course, is that I'm slightly delirious through lack of sleep. I think this is perhaps the intersection where what we call 'the supernatural' comes into being: a combination of weather, the visions of abnormally tired people with big imaginations, and an environment where not too much technology or science can infringe. Once you get on top of your sleep, and bring progress and electricity-based frivolity into the picture, the supernatural is banished.

Was I inviting this idea of the supernatural by coming here, alone? Of course I was. I wanted to live in a place without too many explanations, where magic has a chance to breathe. Chloe could never have lived in a place like this. She struggled to live in a place half like this. She avoided the margins, the fuzzy areas. Enjoyed convenience, firm answers about the week ahead. Or – if you look at it another way – did not like to make life hard for herself. This morning, I saw Mr Conkleton go past the window, dragging his bad foot after him. It is just me and him for a mile, nobody else. He still hasn't fixed the extractor fan, but I didn't go after him. I was too tired. I alternately dozed and read more about the history of

Grindlow. Still no internet. It will be three weeks, at least, the phone company say. Because of Christmas and all. No matter. More room for magic to breathe.

At college I studied printmaking under a great man: a wide, hairy, big-handed chunk of human bread named Malcolm. He is long dead now. In his spare time, Malcolm carved the most exquisite forest creatures out of wood that he had foraged himself from parts of the South Downs near his home. The last time I ever saw him, on my twenty-fifth birthday, he gave me a wooden owl, and it has accompanied me to every house I've lived in since. Before I'd found a spot for almost anything else here, I placed it on the window ledge of the study, but tonight I noticed it had fallen into the wastepaper basket beneath the desk. This was clearly the work of Nibbler, who is getting antsy since I haven't quite had the confidence to let her out to roam yet. I returned the owl to its rightful place on the window ledge. There is another owl carved on the gatepost of the house and I have to admit this is something that first drew me to the place: I thought the two could be companioned. I am reminded here of something Chloe once said to me during an argument: 'Why don't you just fuck off and write a book about owls or something?' She was very angry at the time and later apologised, and promised she didn't mean it. But I actually don't think it was a terrible suggestion. There are far worse activities a person can partake in than fucking off and writing a book about owls or something.

12 DECEMBER

I moved here because of the wildness of the place, but I also underrated that wildness, perhaps because it is not an edge place. It is not at the end of anywhere. If you drive in any direction from here, before long you will hit a city, and when the cities do appear, they appear abruptly, full of industry and smoke. But it is wild. Behind my back garden, sloping down to the valley, are 300 acres of natural woodland: an undisturbed place, somehow simultaneously overgrown and barren, which I could probably walk for the next month and still not fully know. The skeletons of giant hogweed stand proud, despite the snow, beside a ruined pump house. So much vegetation here smacks of death effigy. Beyond is a horizon where nothing grows. I am starting to feel ringed by something here, something more than snow, something ice hot, but I don't know what it is. I see it in my mind when I think about where I can go, what I can do, when the snow goes.

It is a barrier, bigger than the snow itself, which stops me getting into the car and reaching the road.

13 DECEMBER

It couldn't have worked out between me and Chloe. In the end, there were too many differences in what we wanted out of our futures. But am I allowed to say I miss her? One of the things I miss most is the way we fitted together, physically. I don't simply mean in a sexual sense. I mean that all our shapes were right. We'd just fold and melt into each other. It wasn't one of those relationships where you found your arm or leg sticking out somewhere inconvenient and yearned to move it. I also miss the sound of her talking to herself, or talking to a cat, in a distant room of the house. I still find myself listening for it here. Peter Winfield has been over with some firewood. He is such a kind man.

15 DECEMBER

The cats have been going into the garden for a couple of days now, but they don't seem interested in being out there for long. There's been a break in the snow and a small thaw, which has opened up patches of soil for them to piss and shit in, and meant that today I was able to risk a drive to Buxton to get food. It's a town that once seemed high and windbeaten to me – an outpost a little above the world – but seems soft and low now, in context of my new life. I returned and couldn't find Nibbler, who, I realised, after several worried hours, has discovered a gap at the back of the boiler room, leading to a small recessed space where it is warm to sleep. Before that I'd spent an hour outside, calling her name fruitlessly into the black wind. It feels like the night out there has fangs. Through the gloom I can see the branches of the double sycamore man-tree flailing at the sky. Beyond it are untold numbers of old bones from a different universe, but bones that in fact did their growing only thirteen or fourteen generations from where we are now. There is far, far more mould in the bathroom than I realised. I opened up the cistern today and found thick black goo, with dozens of slugs floating in it. The wind is whuooop-whuoooping furiously through the hood of the cooker. Four months tomorrow I begin my new job in the History department at the university. By then, there'll be new growth and all this white around will be green. Or will it? It doesn't seem possible.

Ghosts are weather.

17 DECEMBER

Matthew, who was breaking up a journey to Scotland where he was attending a conference, came to visit yesterday. He parked the car at the top of the track and I trudged up through the snow to meet him. We had a fair bit to talk about, as I hadn't had chance to say goodbye to him properly before I left Sussex: mostly him filling me in on what had happened on campus since my departure. He commented that the house was amazing and that I was pretty much 'living in the eighteenth century', but I thought I saw a few questions in his eyes, and I know he feels that I abandoned him a little with my abrupt departure. He produced his hand lens as we passed the footpath sign pointing to Wentworth's Well and analysed the light green lichen stuck to the wood, which he informed me was a kind of Cladonia.

The sign is incorrect. Wentworth – first name Richard – is not in fact well; he died in 1712, long after he had finished his stint as the reverend of Grindlow. But in the 1660s, when the plague hit the village to such devastating effect, having arrived from London in a box of cloth sent to a local tailor, Wentworth did stay well while his parishioners died: dozens of them each month. It was his decision to seal the village in, to prevent the spreading of the disease to neighbouring Derbyshire villages, for which he is remembered as a hero, but which many of the residents might not have felt quite so positive about at the time. In the hot summer of 1666 the contagion increased, and seventy-four villagers died in that July alone, including Wentworth's wife and two-year-old baby son. Residents of the neighbouring village, Hatherford, left food at a number of sites around the edge of Grindlow, including the spring that was later named after the reverend. For payment, Grindlow villagers left coins. These they soaked in vinegar, as a rudimentary form of sterilisation.

Matthew asked me how the book was going and I admitted I had not yet written a sentence of it. There is plenty of time until I'm back in a full-time teaching job and I feel that a period of faffing is an important part of any big, intense piece of writing, but I had hoped I'd have got properly under way with the book by now. I have a mental barrier with it not unlike the mental barrier that makes me feel that the world beyond the snow and the hills is far away and inaccessible. I told Matthew about the ghost cat – which remained quiet for the duration of his stay – and the carved owl falling into the bin. After he'd left and I'd stripped the bed in the spare room, I noticed that he'd thrown it back in there, just to wind me up, the bastard.

19 DECEMBER

Christmas is out there somewhere, beginning to happen. I am glad to be away from it. Not it so much as the stuff around it. The needless panic, the commercial excess, the small talk centred around the needless panic and commercial excess. I imagine Chloe is out there in it, somewhere. I picture her with a Christmas Person, introducing him to her parents. He doesn't work in academia. He is helping to wash up and decorate the tree, and makes his own signature drink, which everyone enjoys. He has some books, but only five or six – not the amount of books that might become an impediment when you're in a relationship with a person. Everyone – not excluding me – is so relieved to see her finally with a Christmas Person.

She's not in my dreams so much any more, but I dream a lot here. Often, but not always, in the dreams, great violence is about to be done to me. In the most recent, I was walking down a corridor, fumbling for a light switch in impossible blackness. As I reached for the wall for some balance, I felt three fleshless hands violently tickling my ribs. When I wake from these nightmares and I switch my phone on to look at the time, it is always 3.46 or 3.47 a.m. I suspect that once, many years ago, at

3.44 a.m., something very bad happened in this house or in the space where this house now stands. Sometimes when I can wake up, I hear the phantom-cat – or rats, or is it a dog? – noise but it seems a little less keening now, calmer.

20 DECEMBER

Walked to Hatherford today and bought twenty-four packets of crisps. Nineteen of them still exist.

21 DECEMBER

Solstice. White and hard and sharp. It's over a week since I wrote to Conkleton about the slugs and the mould – also reminding him about the extractor fan – but there has been no response. The shower has started leaking and scalded my thigh yesterday. Water is pouring from the broken rear gutter. I saw him out on the track tonight when I'd emerged from the shower, but by the time I had gone to find him, he had vanished. He doesn't move quickly, with that bad foot of his, so I walked in the direction of the big house, sure that I would catch him up. It's a much larger version of my house: same high ceilings, soot-grey bricks and thick walls. Another owl – the same as the one on my gatepost; a little ugly, if I'm honest – is carved on the arch above the door. Peter Winfield has told me that it's the family crest: 'Reet proud of it he is, too. He's got blazers wi' it on.'

There were no lights on, although the curtains were open, and I could see a huge manger set up in the living room. I know Conkleton is religious, but I wonder why he'd go to this effort: Peter Winfield told me Conkleton's wife died three years ago and that his only remaining relative is his son, who lives in New Zealand, and doesn't tend to visit. Despite the darkness of the house, something told me somebody was there, so I checked on the kitchen side. Peering through the kitchen into the dining room beyond, I could just see a figure that appeared to be Conkleton, standing against the back wall. I knocked on the window, but I couldn't get his attention. It was as if he was in some kind of trance, pinned to the spot. I did not think he was in any serious danger, though, so I trudged back home. I am so tired and I think I might have a problem with my Achilles tendon. Perhaps everyone gets foot injuries around here? When I arrived home, Matthew called to ask if he'd left one of his turquoise rings anywhere in my spare room. I said I would look, and told him that he was a wanker for putting the owl in the bin. He told me he had no knowledge of any such thing.

28 DECEMBER

This place – this part of the Peak District – has its own particular winter smell. It followed me on a walk today: a very long one. It's different from any smell I've smelt while walking anywhere else. There is almost nothing of my former home in it. It's a little woodsmoky, but also tinged with manure and mournful old stone and a hint of Victorian industry. I feel different while within this smell. People are expected to be the same person all their life, but different places make us different people. I'm not talking about the impact of an environment over time; I'm talking about something instantaneous. My hair is different here, my outlook, even my face, maybe. I am more lethargic, which is unlike me. I don't sleep fully, though, because of the nightmares at 3.44 and my active mind.

I dozed and read and snacked through the festive season, as many people will do, the notable difference being that I did it all alone. For my Christmas meal, I had a bagel smeared with Marmite. I did not mind. It was a very pleasant bagel.

Yesterday I decided the solution to my insomnia is to physically exhaust myself. I walked down the valley, below the snowline, into the limestone gorge, until I was nine full miles away from home, over the border from Dark Peak into White and only by turning around and retracing my steps could I make it back before nightfall. A few festive family walking parties shuffled about nearer the road, but mostly I was alone. I slipped on limestone and fell on top of my camera, amazingly neither breaking it nor me. White Peak limestone makes for less bleak hills than the gritstone of the Dark Peak, but it always feels like it's getting away from you. In the winter, nothing ever feels certain in life when you're on top of it. I will do well not to perish as a result of it before spring arrives. Shaken, I passed through a gate, noting the top section of a freshly decapitated deer on the path in front of me: the work, no doubt, of poachers. Its face stayed with me. I could feel the bruise I'd sustained through falling, but as I progressed on the walk, my Achilles pain dissipated.

I got home and sank into a deep bath and thanked myself for changing the sheets in the morning. They felt good against my skin and as I turned and snuggled hard to Chloe, I was reminded of how seamlessly our bodies – my long one, and her tiny one – slotted together against the odds.

I noticed she did not emanate her usual warmth, though. There was purring at the bottom of the bed, near our feet.

'You're so cold,' I said.

'Can't help it. Always been that way,' Chloe said, in what was not her voice.

I turned on the light. The bed was empty. The purring had stopped. The top of the room seemed very large and wastefully utilised.

It's morning now, and I am benefiting from the novelty of not having woken up from a nightmare at 3.44 a.m. I do not feel alone in the house, though. I don't think I ever have.

2 JANUARY

I have been thinking more about Winifred Cowlishaw and the Cowlishaw graves. What must it have taken to have done that, bury your whole family, alone, in the space of one week? The question is not how you recover from that, because surely you don't. The question is how you find a way to carry on and be in the world, even a different world, with very different standards of hardship and suffering from those we have now. The route into the village by road or footpath is deceptive and makes the graves seem far away, but as the crow flies they're less than half a mile from here. The cottage beside them, where the Cowlishaw family lived, is long demolished, but were I in this house in the seventeenth century, we'd have pretty much been next-door neighbours: all that lies between us is Conkleton's place and the untamed, slaloming woodland beyond it. Nothing has come into that space since, not even one of the lead or fluorspar mines that dominate the area.

On my walk today I saw five dead moles nailed to a fence. 'It's showin' off, trophyism, a warning,' Winfield has told me. He traps and kills them himself, but just to keep their hills under control. He says he'd never do something like that. I told him about the night I saw Conkleton pinned to the wall. He did not look surprised. Winfield said he tries not to go down there. I looked at his face again and saw more weather. It's an excellent face. Looking good for your age and looking young for your age are often not the same thing.

The village shop is stocking a new jalapeño snack. The four bags I have consumed so far have been quite addictive. These things are often just sold for a trial period, so it's good to be supportive.

Crows are fucking massive here.

6 JANUARY

This is just a diary and I suspect (in fact, hope) nobody else will ever read it, so – with the knowledge that I'm going to sound like I've totally lost it – I might as well come out and say this: I have been hearing the female voice – the one I heard when I thought I felt Chloe beside me in bed – again. I don't understand everything it says. The words are thick, very North Derbyshire, but also more than just very North Derbyshire. A lot of what the voice says is a mixture of the banal and the incomprehensible. It has asked a couple of times if I am OK. It was only today that I replied for the first time to something it said. I was in bed at the time.

'Reckon 'im be bringing down the white again tonight.'

'You mean it's going to snow?'

'Yuss.'

12 JANUARY

What I decided before I came here was that I wanted to write a book about four children, all of whom had starred in a 1960s TV series and subsequently become friends for life. The novel would be about the very different paths they had taken since, the narrative returning with an update every four years. For a long time I ached to write it, felt nothing about my life would be calm and right until I did. I saw being here, this period before I start my job at the university, as my chance to finally do it. Two years ago, I'd have auctioned a close relative for this freedom. But I have still not written a word. I suspect its window has gone and I might have to just accept that. The motor beneath the project is no longer there. I have written since arriving here, but only in the form of this diary, and notes I have made on Grindlow's history from the books I have purchased.

Today I read about Benjamin Rowley, a farm lad who lived in Grindlow during the 1660s, and Hannah Barlow, his lover, who lived in Hatherford. Each day the pair would meet at 2 p.m. at the exact halfway point between the villages and stand a hundred yards apart, staring longingly at each other, yearning for the time when the pestilence would pass and they would once again be properly reunited. For thirteen weeks the routine continued, until one day Benjamin did not appear, and Hannah instantly knew that the worst had happened. The following day, she attempted to throw herself from the top of the gorge but her expanding petticoats broke her fall, meaning she emerged only with light bruising.

She eventually lived until eighty-two, having married a butcher from Hatherford.

'Knew her daughter, I did,' said the voice, as I closed the book. 'She were right loose.'

Conkleton has finally been over about the slugs and the mould and the leak and the fan. He does not look well. I told him I'd show him where the problem was and invited him in. He remained on the threshold and told me it wasn't necessary. He said he would send somebody over to fix it.

16 JANUARY

I am getting out a little more in the car, in these days where the snow has turned more patchy, but not going far. I still feel that invisible threshold stopping me. I do not dare go on a proper day trip, never want to get back too late. I don't like leaving the cats on their own as they're still jittery, but I also feel the house as a stone presence inside me that cannot be neglected for long. I edge up the hill, coming the back way, nervous of black ice. I have skidded a couple of times. It never doesn't seem like an achievement to make it to the top. Sometimes I see hares skittering across the icy fields. I put the rubbish out today and lost my footing. I stayed upright only by grabbing on to the rear windscreen wiper of my car. It part-survived. It still cleans half of the rear windscreen.

There are ledges to the land here. There is the ledge that you think is high, where the weather changes, where a day can be entirely different from the way it is down in the valley. Then there is the ledge above that. Sometimes I'm driving along the main road and I look up at those higher ledges and wonder what kind of crazy person would live up there, then remember the answer is me.

She says her name is Catherine.

21 JANUARY

I remember that this was the time of year where I felt it all turn over, back in Sussex. The first daffodils would be out, maybe a few primroses, even. There are snowdrops down near the river now, but not many. I have been online and found myself searching for photographs of this place in spring and summer, in need of hard evidence of their existence. My firebowl is in the garden, where the movers left it. It is half full of snow. Its existence is pure comedy. I can't foresee any time I will get to use it.

Walking back from Grindlow with a multipack of pickled onion Space Raiders, I noticed an odd wooden shape built into the wall of a cottage – probably early 1800s – on the east side of the village. I realised on closer inspection that it was an old pillory. You initially read the story of Grindlow and you get an impression of friendliness and support from the other population centres in the vicinity – the food left at the wells, and the boundary stones, an acknowledgement of the selflessness that Wentworth instilled – but it's not that simple. Long after the plague had passed, residents were often treated with suspicion. Grindlow residents who attempted to enter Sheffield were still often pelted with pebbles and sharp sticks. Until well into the 1700s it was thought of as extremely bad luck to let a Grindlow woman near your sheep or cattle.

24 JANUARY

Outside, the night has fangs again. I felt it in my gums as I put food out for the birds, who are desperately hungry. A long icicle has formed on the gatepost, under the carved owl: a potential disposable murder weapon. If it wasn't for the floodlight on Winfield's barn, there'd be nothing to light up this night for over a mile. The wind keeps setting the floodlight off, and it illuminates the snow, meaning a rhombus of white-yellow brightness comes through the gap in the bedroom curtains. There is purring in the bottom-left corner of the room, where I can't see. I am not quite asleep when I hear her.

'Feel better. Now that you're here.'

'Why?'

'Make me stronger. Didn't like last winter. Felt lonely.'

'What about summer?'

'Wasn't here. Never am.'

'Not at all?'

'No.'

'Where were you?'

'I don't know.'

'What about in autumn?'

'Some of it.'

'Spring?'

'Some of it.'

'You have never been back in the bed, after that first time.'

'Not fair. Not fair on you. Not fair on me.'

28 JANUARY

It was Mark Avery who first alerted me to the job in Sheffield at the university. We'd kept in touch ever since my early days working at ULU. He's a smooth-cheeked, boyish man, still terrified of relationships at thirty-seven, flick-quiffed, eternally excitable about sport. He's been trying to get me out for a drink ever since I arrived in the Peak but it's been difficult, with the snow and everything. Yesterday, though, I got the train from Hatherford and met him for a pint on the leafy margins of the city. He asked me what Grindlow was like, and said he'd heard it was kind of dark. The booze went to my head pretty quickly, so when he told me he and his new girlfriend, Carla, were going out to a gig on the other side of town, I took little persuading to join them. She's a few years younger than him and plays in an all-female punk band.

Later, after the band had finished and the DJ took over, my energy was still up – higher than it had been for weeks – and the rest of Carla's bandmates arrived, each of them heavily eye-shadowed and immaculate in gaudy patterned dresses. A glam-punk look that is heavily in debt to the past but not quite of it. 'This is Jeff – he lives in a haunted house!' Mark barked over the music, by way of introduction. I got talking to Rosie, the drummer, who works part time in a new bakery in town and was at least 50 per cent covered in sequins, and soon there were shots and she was asking me if I was single. I told her I was. 'I'm not really looking for anything at the moment, though,' I burbled. 'I'm pretty happy as I am. Also, I'm a little broken.' At which point, with the assertive statement, 'You're not broken – nobody is broken,' she planted a confident, lingering kiss on my lips.

It was a long time before any taxis arrived outside the venue, and while we waited Rosie made some practical and persuasive arguments for me to not try to get back to Grindlow and to stay at her place instead: the fact that Mark and Carla had long since vanished into the night; the black ice on the lane leading up to the top of the mountain; the comfiness of the new memory-foam mattress on the bed of her flatmate, who was currently in Greece; the breakfasts at the new vegan café at the end of her road. I kissed her once more, gave her my number, and put her in the first cab that arrived. I had to wait another three quarters of an hour before I found a taxi that would agree to take me to where I live, and even then, when we climbed the mountain itself, he refused to take me up to the final ledge. 'Never in January, mate,' he said. 'Not a chance. You'll not find one cabbie in this city who'll take you up there.' I stumbled and skidded and sloshed my way home, bidding a final farewell to my suede boots in the process.

I woke less than four hours later to the agonised sounds of one of Winfield's cattle giving birth. My clothes, which I'd left strewn about the landing, were in a neat pile outside my bedroom door. The bird feeders were both empty, so I went outside to top up their feed, my head rattling in my skull. There was still a little bit of snow in the firebowl. The carved owl sat neatly on top of it.

29 JANUARY

'Are you angry?' I ask her. We're in the kitchen. Me: washing the pots. Her: somewhere less specific, mostly in the underutilised top part of the room.

'No.'

'Are you sure?'

'Yuss. Not with you. Always angry, though. A bit.'

'Will you tell me about it sometime? I'd like it if you did.'

'Maybe. Yuss.'

'And what about the owl?'

'Don't like it.'

'You don't like owls?'

'Yuss. No. Yuss.'

'You just don't like representations of owls in art?'

'Yuss.'

4 FEBRUARY

Two of Winfield's lambs died today. It is nothing unusual for him, at this time of year, but it's still deeply sad. In the coldest March of recent years he arrived one morning to find all his sheep facing the wall, and an entire field of their offspring frozen to death. He is hardened to it, but I still impulsively asked him if he fancied going into the village for a pint. I've not asked before, as I always assume he's working too hard for that kind of thing, and that after a day on the farm all he wants to do is get back home to his wife and his boys. But he surprised me by accepting.

Behind us at the bar a fat-necked racist bemoaned the multicultural shops on his recent trip to London, and joke-seriously chided his drinking companion for not looking into his eyes as they clinked glasses. A little threat sizzled in the air around them. The bar room smelt of meat and damp and wood. Winfield talked about the 'shit weather corridor' we are in here, which comes down from the north, and often manages to miss the flanking villages and hills, or at least never hit them nearly as hard. He'd heard next week was going to be bad, and was making a new warm space in the barn for the lambs. He said that whenever he meets someone new he looks at their hands to see if they're small, which can be useful at lambing time. It's an ingrained habit, hard to stop. 'How did you rate mine?' I asked. 'Didn't quite make the grade, I'm afraid, yoth,' he replied. He said I was doing well up there. Some of the other tenants who'd come up here in winter hadn't even managed to hack it this long: they'd gone to stay with relatives, or left altogether.

When Winfield returned from the bar with our second pint, he was accompanied by a much older man, with enormous sideburns. He introduced him as Norman, his dad. Norman farmed for years on the other side of the ridge and looks how I assumed farmers ceased to look in about 1965. He is eighty-three – older than I'd taken him for – and has lived in the area all his life. He was a first-hand witness to the Grindlow air crash in the terrifyingly cold winter of 1947; listened to the plane go over his head in the fog, then the impact. 'You could hear t'ice cracking everywhere in t'trees that year,' he said. 'When you took your coat off it stood up all by itsen.' Had he met my landlord? 'Aye, I've met him. He's not a proper person. Woke up from t'first day with everything and never learned how to appreciate it. Bad news, that family. Always 'ave been. Owned everything round 'ere for ever. Course, it's just him now, after she died, a few years back. There's his son, too, but he won't come back from abroad. Don't know what will happen to the place after he's gone.'

8 FEBRUARY

Phone call from my mum, who wants to know why I have posted her a carved owl covered in bubblewrap. I told her it wasn't permanent, just for safekeeping. 'Could it not have waited?' she asks. She said she is worried about me, up here, all alone. I told her it's no big deal. What about people in the northern provinces of Canada? What about people on mountains in Scotland, in January, in the seventh century?

Text message from Mark, inviting me to a pub quiz in Sheffield. I decline. I am worried about this weather that's coming in. Just little flurries of snow so far, but the top ledge of the mountain road is still dicey from the last lot. The council's attitude to gritting seems to be that over a certain altitude it should be done on a self-serve basis. Catherine is quiet today but, I sense, more peacefully so. It's a month and a half since solstice, but the day is still a slit of light, bookended by big black cushions.

10 FEBRUARY

I saw them through the back window, coming up over the ridge, with their dogs and guns. A Good Size Cat was out there and I hurried him in quickly. Locked the cat flap. I couldn't quite see what they were carrying: rabbits, certainly, something longer, stringier, maybe a hare. I moved to the front of the house, keen to get confirmation of their departure. Their faces were hard and sharp. They lingered around the barns for a while, talking to Conkleton. He stuck around for a few minutes after they left, stroking gates, inspecting barns, ostentatiously showing to himself that everything was still in order, like a friendless child playing at being king. He steered noticeably clear of this place.

'Is he scared of you?' I asked her.

'He's scared of it all. Scared of himself.'

'Do you ever go to his house, too?'

'Sometimes. But that's Joan's territory.'

'Joan?'

'Sister.'

13 FEBRUARY

The fog is marauding on the other side of the valley this morning, angry and rampant. Sometimes it will be there for three or four whole days without lifting. But if you looked back from there to this side, it would no doubt be thicker. When I've walked over there and the view has been clear, it's amazing how hidden this place is. The system of ledges and copses makes the spot almost impossible to pick out. It's a vast valley that has totally redefined the word 'hill' for me. I find myself thinking a lot about all that wild ground in the middle, where the derelict pump house is. It's been so left to itself that it has brewed its own atmosphere. The hunters – and me – are really the only people who go down there. I don't like the thought of them doing their shooting, asserting their bullshit supremacy, but I don't think they are winning. I think the valley is still winning. It has too much strength. It is a primeval strength that scares me, but the fear is different from my other common fears: the prospect of getting a speeding ticket, or hurting a person's feelings, or falling terminally ill, or losing a loved one. It's an important and timeless and necessary fear, with no anxiety associated with it.

15 FEBRUARY

'I haven't asked you about the cat.'

'Not mine. Came with the house.'

'But I assumed, what with . . .'

'That's just it. People assume too much. Life's big problem.'

I resist the urge to add, '. . . and death's?' I don't want to be rude.

17 FEBRUARY

The house was built in 1837. I have decided that it happened in winter but have no evidence that it did, other than the fact that winter has become all I associate this area with, and the actual raw materials of the house were blatantly picked out with the kind of winters you get up here in mind. The building probably seemed a little show-offy at the time, purely due to the size of its rooms, but in a dour way that mirrors the meteorological environment: it's a house that smacks of gritting your teeth and toughing it out, of scant humour, all of it black. A blizzard pelted the walls tonight and I was glad of their thickness, as almost two centuries of residents before me must also have been. This spell of extreme weather – or rather, even *more* extreme weather – has been longer in coming than we were informed on the news, but it has not been overhyped. The cats – the two I can see as a corporeal presence, anyway – look genuinely bewildered.

The scene outside the front door is as frightening as something pristine can be. My car is totally invisible, a lump of snow notable only for being larger than nearly all the other lumps of snow around it. The flakes are still falling. They're not even flakes. They're ready-made snowballs.

I have worked it out, and I think I have ten days' worth of food, if I go easy on the crisps. I can feel Catherine watching me as I cook. She sees me make space amidst the fresh chillis, peppers and tomatoes and carefully drop my eggs into the pan, and I can tell she finds it all a bit needless and elaborate. I've noticed that she's talking in a different way: her sentences are clearer. I wonder if it's from speaking to me a lot, listening to me on the phone, or hearing the radio. I have got into the habit of leaving Radio 4 on for her while I'm out. By the looks of it, she won't hear Radio 4 for a while.

19 FEBRUARY

I thought today of a story I overheard in the post office during my first few days here. A lady from the village – she must have been at least in her mid-eighties – was talking about one winter here in her youth when the snow was so extreme that she and her husband could only get down the hill for food by crawling through the drifts on their hands and knees. It seemed preposterous at the time, an exaggerated recollection from an unrecognisable age. Today I can believe it. I've just been out to do the bins and the birdseed and it's like a whole different planet out there. The dark white light of December and January is history. Now it's all blasted silver. Your whole body squints as you fight your way through it. The double sycamore man-tree looks like it's drowning, not raging, as it waves its endless arms at the sky. The relief as you shut the front door on it is monstrous.

We keep the fire going all day with more of Winfield's wood, and we tell each other stories. She tells me the cat prefers Joan to her.

'Does it have a name?' I ask.

'Cat,' she says.

21 FEBRUARY

When she tells me her surname I immediately realise I knew it all the time. 'Not . . .?' I reply. 'No,' she says. 'Daughter?' I say. 'Granddaughter,' she replies. Not all of the children died in that Satanic week in that most Satanic of years, 1666 – that's what people forget. One baby – Josephine – lived and, with her, Winifred carried on. It was sympathy and support that kept her in the village, stopped her from starting a new life elsewhere, which might have been a more sensible option. Neighbours cooked and washed for her. But over the years sympathy gradually thawed out, then froze into suspicion – much more coldly by the time Winifred had died, and Josephine was living with two young daughters of her own. It was less about the Cowlishaws than it was about the village itself: its need to unshackle itself from its own recent past. When residents visited other places, there was name-calling, a stigma, a taint. A grudge seemed to be held, even though it made no sense. Surely the surrounding villages should hold the opposite of a grudge, after the suffering that Wentworth had saved them from, with his decision to seal Grindlow off? But it felt like a new, harder, less forgiving era.

'Even then?' I ask.

'Even then,' she says.

How, I wonder, can eras always do this, keep seeming harder and less forgiving than the previous one, yet never reach a peak, unsurpassable hardness, without mercy or kindness?

People looked at Catherine and Joan, and they were reminded of the plague years. It didn't help that illness was their speciality. They'd learned the remedies from Josephine, as she had learned them from Winifred before that. What comfrey can do to help to heal broken bones. The relationship between nettles and the blood. How to apply yarrow to a cut. People had a conflicted relationship to the cottage on the hill, outside the village, a steaming, pungent house full of medicated goo. They went there for poultices and remedies, but they often kept quiet about it. In spring Catherine and Joan headed through the woods to the stream bordering the big farm. Sometimes trespassing was necessary to get to the places where the Lady's Smock and ramsons grew most abundantly, but what was trespassing? Then was not now, with its Ordnance Survey order. Paths were a debate.

The sisters were spotted a few times, but it never really mattered until one year early in the new century, when several of the Conkleton cattle were struck down. It was a harsh, late dragging winter, where almost nothing came up in the hedgerow. Lambs died in more abundance than ever. Then the son, the big family favourite, the one born into it all with so much to lose, out riding on the sharp bit of the ridge, was flung. It was later agreed that the mare in question would not have flung anyone, least of all him, not under normal circumstances. There was no way it could happen. The body was not found until the next day. Blood had soaked the front of his blazer. An owl, once all grey, was half red.

23 FEBRUARY

The absolute coldest. They say −16°C, with windchill. And that's at the edge of the village. I think you could safely take away another three degrees from that, up here on the ledge. I am using my laptop to heat my feet: a second, electronic hot-water bottle, to add to the one on my lap. Winfield's wood has all gone, and I do not want to trouble him for more. He's coming up here every day still, but only to check on the sheep in the barn. No way you can work in this. I have not seen Conkleton for days. I have replied to only two of the text messages I have received during the last week: the one from my dad, asking if I am OK up here on the mountain, and the almost identical one from my mum, also asking if I am OK up here on the mountain. I will get around to responding to the others soon, when I have a moment. They are as follows.

1. *Just wanted to say it was really nice meeting you the other day. Let me know if you fancy a coffee when you are next in Sheffield. Rosie x*

2. *Hey fella. Wanted to check you are ok out there. It is pretty bad here right now and I heard it's worse where you are. Please holler if you need anything. Mark.*

3. *Your latest O2 bill is now available to view online.*

4. *Shit. It must be pretty scary up there right now. Hope you are OK. Matthew.*

5. *Open mic tonight at café in Nether Edge. Might wander up. You're probably snowed in, out there in the haunted house, but just thought I'd mention it. Rosie.*

25 FEBRUARY

Found a jar of olives at the back of the mug cupboard. Result! In less salutary news, I cannot eke out the cat litter any longer. Nibbler and A Good Size Cat are refusing to go and do their business outside, so I have been out with the shovel, cleared some snow, and scraped some frozen soil into their tray. They will just have to use that, when the ice drips off it, until I can venture out again in the car, if that ever happens.

'What do you think of the world now?' I ask her.

'It's the same.'

'Surely you can't think that? So much has changed. So much progress.' I hold up my phone: still switched off, as it has been for the last thirty hours.

'Humans are still the same.'

'You think so?'

'They still need something to hate. They still operate in packs. They repeat sayings, like sheep. When something is said about someone enough times by enough people, it becomes a fact, whether it is true or not.'

'What about the cottage? Is it still there?'

'No. Not even a brick.'

'Was it here? Where we are now?'

'No. Half a mile.'

'So why are you here instead?'

'You ask a lot of questions. Men didn't, in my day.'

'So people are different, after all?'

27 FEBRUARY

There has been a thaw over the last day. I can see a central dividing line of meltwater coming down the track. But it's creating a new kind of slippiness, on top of the ice. I do not think I will attempt to get in the car yet. Winfield's dad has been here, helping him with the lambs. He brought me a casserole made by his wife. I did not have the heart to tell him I don't eat meat. We could see some snowdrops just showing their heads above the ice on the side of the track, beneath the wire fence.

'They're amazing things,' he observed. 'They'll thrive under snow and ice, but if it's warm and dry, they won't grow. You can't tell me that can be explained. That's not just nature. There's something more going on there.'

My foot aches and my hair is a pile of straw.

1 MARCH

They came for them at the last moment that dusk was still dusk, carrying burning sticks. Around thirty in total, two of them on horseback at the helm. All men, except for one near the rear. The man on the front horse wore a jacket with an owl sewn into it. She hadn't been ready – neither of them had – but when it happened, she felt a wave of acceptance come over her, like she had known all along that it was coming.

Joan struggled more. Jars and pots were kicked over. A chunk of her hair could still be seen on the floor weeks later, until sparrows finally forged their way in through the hole in the roof and used it for their nest. By 4 a.m. it was all over. It ended on the top of the hill, and the light from the fire was such that she could see right down the valley to the new big house, whose walls were now almost complete. The man who was going to live there had once come to her at night with stomach pains, and she had sent him away with a remedy. He had not been back, so she had made the deduction that it had been successful.

'Why don't I meet her? Joan?'

'You have. She's different from me. She doesn't talk. She has been here less lately.'

'My nightmares?'

'Yuss.'

'I'm so tired all the time.'

'I'm sorry. My fault, a bit. You won't be, soon.'

5 MARCH

It's different down in the valley. It's hard to explain exactly how it works to somebody who's not lived up here. A person who knew that I'd moved here might drive along the river road and think, 'This is where Jeff lives,' but they'd be incorrect. I live on top of the mountain and that is a different thing. I could live in an entirely different country, and it might have more in common with the valley than this place does. Down there the big freeze is already a distant memory. People are sitting on the rocks in the woodland, eating pots of yoghurt, with their sleeves rolled up. A woodpecker is doing a roll on its wooden drum to herald the lighter days. Up here, though, the fangs in the air remain. Snow bones are clinging stubbornly to the fields. The light is still dark white. I watch the forecast, anxiously, every day.

Yesterday, Mark and Carla arrived unannounced with a huge Le Creuset pot of homemade soup. 'Bloody hell! Grizzly Adams!' said Mark, as I opened the door. I think I might have talked too much, expending all my stored-up voice. Carla mentioned her friend was leaving a two-bed terrace on the north-west side of Sheffield, which was up for rent. 'Not that I'm assuming you'd be looking,' she said. 'We just thought in some ways it might be easier.' She said it was a very up-and-coming neighbourhood. Some great pubs. Rosie lived just around the corner, too. Did I remember Rosie? I said I did, then asked them if they knew the actual statistics for how many Grindlow villagers died in 1666: an average of twenty-one per week. Twenty-one! When they had left, the house felt very quiet. Catherine is out, I think.

7 MARCH

More blackbirds are arriving every day. I can't get the seeds and fat balls out there for them quick enough. I remember the first day I came here and explored the village. I stood outside the pub, consulting my map and noticed a blackbird puffed up, beside my feet, quivering. I walked on. I have often looked back and felt there was something I should have done at that moment. But what? 'Maybe not move to a haunted mountain?' I can hear Matthew saying. When I got back from the village today there was a bag of firewood waiting outside my front door. I thanked Winfield, but he said it had nothing to do with him. Later, when I was closing the living-room curtains, I spotted Conkleton limp by, and, uncharacteristically, he waved.

9 MARCH

'Do you blame him for it?'

'No.'

'But he is in some way part of what happened to you? A remnant of it?'

'Yes.'

'And you'll be here until he's gone?'

'We'll be here after that. That doesn't end it.'

'So you're not here to hurt him?'

'No. That's not why we're here. We will always be here. We need to be.'

'It's not revenge, then?'

'It's much more complicated than that. But we have to be here. It's part of the balance. People want simple explanations. That's another one of the big problems in life.'

Again, I resist adding, '. . . and in death?'

11 MARCH

I can picture it quite vividly. It's that glorious intersection of season and sunlight when the leaves throw their warm shapes on the pavements, making them less prosaic places to be. We've been walking for two hours and haven't realised it, and we're in a new corner of the city that neither of us even knew was here. If you looked at it practically, you'd say slow down, don't run out of the good stuff: we've been telling it all too quickly, when really there's months to do it, years maybe. But one topic of conversation leads feverishly to the next. We grab each other's arms a couple of times, and it's pure enthusiasm, nothing affectedly flirty. It's not that we're pretending to like all the same things. We're not that green. But it feels like we're agreeing on the topics we disagree on, because we've established an initial kind of agreement in the angle that we look at everything, and it's making us look at our differences more open-mindedly.

She checks the time and says shit, she has to go, and it already feels painful, the eleven and a half hours until next time, even though this time – the time before next time – isn't yet over. And you know it won't always be like this. It might not even be a quarter like this. Something will come along, an obstacle, maybe not even created by us, and it will make everything harder. But is that a reason not to be here at all, not to even begin?

I turn back to my phone, and delete the text message I have started to compose.

13 MARCH

'Jeff. Oh my God, it's you again. You just will not stop calling, will you?'

'Hi. I'm sorry. I've had a lot on.'

'Consorting with the ghosts? I guess it must be quite hard to get signal up there too, what with that big haunted phone mast at the top of the mountain?'

'So I was wondering. You mentioned a while ago, about maybe doing something. Getting a drink. Might that offer still stand?'

'Hmm. I dunno. I suppose I could bring myself to open the offer up again, despite the fact that you vanished off the face of the earth without saying a word.'

'When would be good for you?'

'Friday isn't too bad.'

I look at the weather on the computer screen in front of me. The yellow symbols.

'Can we say next week? How about Thursday?'

'OK. If you sure you're actually real. Are you a real person? Tell me that, Jeff. Are you? Are you real?'

'I think so. Most of the time.'

15 MARCH

It's coming in again, from the north, straight down the Shit Weather Corridor. I can see it less in the sky and more in the colour of the space between the sky and the ground, and a feeling in the air. It's like when you're in a room and you realise you've left the fridge open, before you've actually checked and got backup visual evidence to prove that the fridge is open. But I can feel that something's turned over, too. Near the dry-stone wall beyond the garden, where some of last week's snow still hides, through the gap in it which weather or sheep or the foot hunt made or some combination of all three made, there's a single primrose. Maybe this will be the last of the snow and, if it's not, the lot after it will be. If I listen closely to my bones, I can know it. I just have to wait it out.

Before the first flurry assaults the north wall of the house, I walk out over the back field, avoiding the really rough bit of ground where the old roots, as if sentient, snag and lick at your legs. There are no public rights of way here, not for another mile. Paths are still a debate. I turn east, up the last bit of hill, to the very highest point of the whole valley. Some of Winfield's sheep are permitted to go semi-nomad up here on the spongy moor turf, feasting on small mountains of hay that steam from their molten core, even in this biting cold. A little blue-orange pouting mouth of light going down over the rock edge on the other side is staving off the gloom. From the top I can see the remains of a Saxon cross, then down the valley, past a vast eighteenth-century manor house, to the kink in the river. I turn back for home and my home comes into view: a big grey monster, bulky and mean and alone. Nobody could have been thinking about calming anybody down when they made it.

Night is coming in now and I've not left any bulbs on. But in the lower window I can see the comforting light from the fire. I will walk towards that orange glow for minutes before any detail about the scene around it emerges. It's just a window gently full of fire. It's a scene that could be from any point in a long, long time. If you'd been dropped here out of nowhere, you'd be able to predict nothing about what else you'd find in there. You'd just see the light, and follow it.

LISTINGS

FOR SALE

Stunning three-bedroom executive home. Would suit professional couple. Woodland views. Jack and Jill bathroom with his 'n' hers sinks. Landscaped garden with ornamental pond. Subterranean enthusiasts please note: unique feature of 'cave' beneath house! Second bathroom with heated towel rail, recessed ceiling lighting and low-level WC. Seller will pay stamp duty for quick move.

TO LET

Three-bedroom executive home. Two bathrooms. Large, attractive garden, backing onto woodland. Strictly no smokers, DSS or pets. The tenant will be required to pay a deposit equivalent to two months' rent, plus an admin fee of £150, plus a checkout fee of £200. Please note that there is no access for tenants to the cave beneath the property.

TO LET

Three-bedroom executive home. Two bathrooms. Large, attractive garden, backing onto woodland. Strictly no smokers, DSS. Pets considered. The tenant will be required to pay a deposit equivalent to one month's rent. No admin fees for December move-in. Please note that there is no access for tenants to the cave beneath the property.

RESIDENCE DESTROYED BY FIRE

In the early hours of Sunday morning a Somerset police and fire rescue team was called to a blaze at a three-bedroom house on the outskirts of the village of Chagdon. Mr Edward Richards and Mrs Charlotte Richards, the tenants of the house, first became aware of the problem when Mrs Richards woke to the smell of smoke and discovered flames licking up from the cellar immediately beneath the house's open-plan Shaker kitchen. Mr and Mrs Richards were able to safely evacuate their two children, Finn and Martha, and no injuries were sustained. Mr Richards then returned to the house to rescue the family's pet labradoodle, Rollo, who was found unconscious in the kitchen, with lacerations to his neck, and is currently in a stable condition at Blackdown Veterinary Practice. The cellar – which according to Mr Richards is 'more like a cavern' – was an original feature of an earlier house on the site, Pepper Farm, which fell into disrepair during the last quarter of the last century, before being redeveloped by the Orchard Homes company, along with much of the west side of Chagdon. The cause of the blaze remains unknown.

LAND FOR SALE

'Limefields'. Build your dream! One-off development opportunity. Quarter-acre of woodland. Edge-of-village location. Good road links. Auction will be held at Chagdon village hall, 3.4.2017. Starting bids of £450,000.

GOBLIN

One of the most fearsome of the West Country goblins is Tunk. Short and hard-bodied, with a wide and sheeplike head, Tunk is said to dwell in various cavernous locations between the Blackdown Hills and the southern reaches of the Mendips, subsisting on hares, dogs, badgers, owls and deer. Often accompanied by sparks and strange clouds of gas, Tunk can seem angry and belligerent on first appearances but is unlikely to do any harm to any human of humble means, provided that at his approach they turn their pockets inside out or find another way to prove to him their lack of wealth. It has been said that Tunk is not a mythical creature at all, but a working medieval farmer who, having been cheated out of his wife and his worldly possessions by a local nobleman, retreated underground to die. Instead of expiring, he continued to age, growing stouter, wartier and fatter-headed with each passing century.

PUB

Take a very short detour to stop at The Gambler's Rest to fortify you for the final climb through ancient woodland to Boggart's Mount. Cask ales are on offer in abundance plus bar snacks and Sunday lunch and a comprehensive vegan menu, all to be enjoyed on the sun terrace or in the unique 'Cavern' area below the main bar. Strictly no dogs.

MISSING PET

None of us have seen our black lab John for three days now. Please inbox us if you have seen him; we are very worried. We was walking him down Bogart's Reach where Gambler's Rest used to be then he went off after his ball an never came back. Suzi x.

THE ARCHITECT CATHERINE SAMUELS

Samuels is tired, like me, from a transatlantic flight when she opens the door of her spacious mountaintop Colorado home, but in the three hours since she got back she has already been out to forage for nettles and a rare strain of orange-berried sagebrush native to the area, both hardy post-Cloud Era survivors, which she uses to make tea for us. She has slender artist's fingers and a longish face that wears a permanent look of slight suspicion, but her complexion and hair are both that of a woman fifteen years her junior. She did not design her own house, which is over ninety years old and of a classic mid-twentieth-century modernist style, but she has made significant alterations to it in her decade here, particularly on the lower floors, which now stretch back further into the rock face.

It is this for which Samuels is best known: creating deep spaces that make an indoor dichotomy of unclean lines feel even more indoors, in an inversion of the more common 'exterior interior', which interacts with a natural unroofed space constructed by nature itself. It was in fact her husband, the actor Michael Gondrum, who found the place, which was roofless and near derelict at the time and occasionally occupied by wolves and brown bears.

'In an ideal world, I'd have gone for something a little darker and closer to sea level, but I like it fine enough,' she tells me in an accent that seems to occupy a fictional landmass, 400 miles west of Ireland.

Was there anything formative in Samuels's childhood that helped develop her taste for underlands? She says she grew up in a succession of fairly dull houses in the south-west of England – 'identikit execuhomes, selling a sub-rural dream while slowly killing any notion of said dream by the very fact of existing' – but does remember one place which 'had a sort of cave in the basement' which, against the wishes of her family, she used to go and play inside.

'My mum told me much later that I used to have a fictional friend down there, who I called "Mr Sheep", but I personally have no recollection of it. I was a very imaginative child, always off on my own, capable of amusing myself in myriad ways. My mum would always say to me, "If you're going anywhere, write it on the kitchen table, so we know." She'd leave a notepad there, but I'd take the instruction literally, and scrawl my whereabouts on the table itself.'

MISSING PET

Pepper. Springer spaniel. Black-and-white markings. Partially deaf. One black ear, one white. Last spotted: Bridgwater Lane area. We have not seen Pepper since early on Saturday evening and we are VERY WORRIED. Our children Jane and and Ben are distraught and would just like their much-loved pup back. Please check your sheds and listen for whimpering near any warrens or badger holes around your property, and report any sightings to us on 01761 563820 or at JimandJules@freedombridge. com.

PARTY

Please help Mephisto and Isobel to celebrate their joint thirtieth birthdays and two decades of wonderful friendship in one of the most beautiful areas of rewilded Somerset. Join in with the dancing, giant Scrabble and a Vietnam battle reconstruction, or just chill out and watch the local wildlife in the swamp and woodland below, including herons, beavers and wild pigs. We have hired out five eco lodges at Boggart Farm and the adjoining campsite and hope to fit everyone in. PLEASE LET US KNOW ASAP if you would like a space in one of the lodges, each of which comes fitted with hot tub and wall-width iFace hook-up screen, and contact Isobel to arrange advance payment. Can't wait to see you all!

OBITUARY

. . . but while his wealth came largely from controversial apps such as Loin Cloth and Celebrity Deathwatch, what Francis will perhaps remain best known for is the pro-hunting marches he organised during the beginning of the last decade, following the re-banning of fox hunting and badger baiting. He later redacted his pro-bloodsport stance, and in the last three years of his life made public donations to several animal rights groups, although remained friends with New Rural Alliance leader Will Park, who was in attendance at the party at which Francis and his husky, Ali, were last seen walking towards an area of reclaimed swampland near Chagdon. Francis remained estranged from his father, the folk musician Ian Francis, until his disappearance. He is survived by his wife, Cheryl, and son, Pontius.

Mephisto Francis (2024–54)

REDEVELOPMENT OPPORTUNITY

Five acres. 'Bogle Marsh View', Chagdon. Potential planning permission to construct new home on site of five existing one-storey dwellings, subject to application.

SWAMP

We park a mile from the swamp and Hendry explains that we must go the rest of the way on foot, before locating the canoe, which he keeps stashed in thick bulrushes on the water's edge. There is arguably no other ecologist who knows this 3,000-acre space as well as he does. He has been charting the wildlife of it since a quarter of it was reclaimed by the floods. He freezes a few yards from the car and puts a finger to his lips. 'It's OK,' he says. 'I thought it was a beaver.' Beavers were only reintroduced to Britain seven decades ago, but there are now thought to be over a thousand living in Somerset's swamps.

We pass just one other example of human life before we reach the kayak: a man in his early seventies, tidying the hedge outside his lone farmhouse. His manner suggests that he and Hendry have met before.

'Got a new friend, Nathan?'

Hendry explains that I am a journalist, here to write about the wildlife of the swamp.

'Hope you've told him about the bogles? I wouldn't stay out after dark if I were you.'

We walk on a few more yards. 'The old folk back in the village will tell you all sorts,' Hendry says, when the man is out of earshot. 'They'll talk about giant eels, and bogles, and boggarts, and a goblin with a sheep's head. Of course, people have gone missing out here. Sometimes they'll bring a dog, and they'll come back to the village without it, but it's all explainable by human folly. People come here to fish and they're unprepared: they don't have a compass and it's easy to get lost. You get little chemical reactions, little gas explosions, on the surface of marsh water like this, and people see it at night and convince themselves they've seen something completely different, straight from their imagination. I've been coming here two decades and I don't think there's a yard I haven't waded through or rowed across and I've not seen anything I can't explain through basic science.'

SPEED AWARENESS

I was one of the first to enter the conference room and I chose a seat in one of the front two rows, as did the other handful of people who had arrived early: all men, apart from me, sipping unenthusiastically at disappointing foyer-coffee-machine coffee and blinking at the light coming through the blinds as if at the realisation that life wasn't what they'd been promised and, at some time not far from now, would be over. A large projector screen awaited us, ominously, a laptop on a table next to it. My uncle arrived about five minutes later and took a seat directly behind me. I turned to look at him in the flesh for the first time in eighteen years.

'All right, Catherine? How do?'

'All right. Yourself?'

'Ticking over nicely. Had a new hot tub installed last weekend on t'terrace.'

'That sounds nice.'

This was one of the main facets I remembered of my uncle's personality from childhood: his unfailing ability to have installed a new, exciting and expensive item in his house every time you visited him. On the few occasions there wasn't a new, exciting and expensive item in his house, there was nearly always a new, exciting and expensive item just outside his house. Cars, usually: dynamically shaped ones.

'Still driving like a nutcase, then?' I asked him. 'Where did you get done?'

'A14. Just past Newmarket, near the new Starbucks. Got a thing on me satnav that tells me where the cameras are but missed the mobile one on the bridge 'cause I were sending a text and they got me doing ninety. You?'

'A143, just outside Ixworth's thirty zone. I was doing thirty-six.'

'Your mum said you was living over here now. Working on trees.'

'You saw her?' I had no knowledge of this.

'Yeah. In IKEA. Was back up in Notts. Went to a concert at the ice rink with Charlotte and bought a bed on the way back.'

I looked through the blinds again, across a lawn covered in worm casts, still four weeks from its first cut of the year. It was February outside in nearly every way. Spring was straining against a natural grey-yellow screen of air. Suffolk light. A path led from the hotel complex to the village church, a Norman one, insulted by every loveless aspect to this building we were in that now blocked its view, insulted by today, by us.

'Expect it keeps you fit,' said my uncle. 'How much does that pay?'

When I'd last seen my uncle at a family party, five full years since the time I'd seen him before that, and not long after I'd got my first job in London, working in publicity for a film company, his opening question to me was, 'How much does that pay?' I had answered him honestly. Now I answered him honestly again.

'Enough.'

'Many women do that sort of thing?'

'A few.'

'How old are you now? Thirty-six?'

'Forty-four.'

'Fuck me. Dunt time fly.'

The door opened and a short man in a lime-green crew-neck sweater entered the room, carrying a brown leather briefcase. I would have put him at about forty-four too, although he had the tissue-paper complexion of someone older, and looked cowed by all light, whether LED or natural. I turned back away from my uncle to face the man in the green crew neck. By this time the room had filled up with six more men who occupied the back two rows and looked a little like my uncle had done when I was a child, and two women, who didn't.

The man in the green crew neck placed his briefcase on the table beside the projector screen and introduced himself as John. He gave a brief outline of the day's timetable, explained that we would have an hour for lunch, which we were welcome to have on or off the premises, and invited us to guess where it was that the most fatalities occurred: motorways, normal A and B roads, or quiet country lanes. People wrote the answer on the slip. The course had only been due to begin two minutes earlier and a few stragglers entered the room and took the remaining seats on the back two rows. John collected the slips and counted them up.

'Only two of you got the right answer,' said John. 'It's quiet country lanes. People crash on quiet lanes less frequently than they do on major roads, but when they do, it takes far longer for emergency services to reach the vehicle. Some people can be trapped, dying, in their vehicle in a field off a quiet country lane for several hours.'

The room vibrated with a low noise.

'Do you think about what it is to die? Or what it is to wait there, dying, but not be able to contact your loved ones, because in the impact of your collision with a tree your spine has been severed, and that means you cannot reach your mobile phone, which keeps ringing, in the footwell of the passenger seat? Or what it is to go on living after you have hit a child at a speed that if it was ten miles slower would not have killed that child?'

A couple of men in the back row laughed, very slightly, but it wasn't a laugh with any humour in it. It was a laugh like a burst crisp packet.

'I look like a dull man to you, I realise,' John continued. 'Some of you will take in what I say, slightly, and change your behaviour, but in a few months your old bad habits will creep in. You will begin to check your phone in the car. You will push the limits, to cut off a bit of time in a journey. But I am telling you the cost, and it is enormous.'

With that he paused, and stared at us. He held the silence. A man on the back row chuckled. The crisp packet again.

'Excuse me for just a second,' said John, and left the room with his briefcase. A minute later I saw him walking across the lawn outside the window towards the church. Nobody else noticed this. Only me, as I was sitting down by the window. As he reached the gate of the church, another man entered the room. He was taller and more confident. He also wore a green crew-neck sweater. He introduced himself as Matt.

'I'm sorry I'm a few minutes late,' said Matt. 'But the

traffic was pretty bad from Ipswich and speeding's not really my thing.'

An air of confusion in the room prevented his joke from really hitting home.

'What happened to John?' asked a man on the back row. Rowdy, an air of Halfords' car park about him. Big neck. Twenty-sixish. Probably ate in Burger King a lot. A seasoned denizen of society's back rows.

'Who's John?' asked Matt.

'The guy who was in here before. We thought he was taking the course.'

'How very strange. I suppose there must have been some mix-up. I don't know of any John, but I'm Matt. Now, I'm sure you're all dying to get this over with so let's begin.'

Matt gave a brief outline of the day's timetable, explained that we would have an hour for lunch, which we were welcome to have on or off the premises, and invited us to guess where it was that the most fatalities occurred: motorways, normal A and B roads, or quiet country lanes. People wrote their answers on slips of paper. Matt was surprised to find that everyone gave the correct answer, and said that it was the first time it had happened in the five years he had been tutoring this course. He told us we were all clearly excellent pupils and moved on, explaining ways we could check what the speed limit was when we were unsure, including looking at the signs on the roads branching off from the road we were on. He made a joke about the drivers in Essex and said that a good way to reduce your speed in villages with 30 mph was to always go down to third as you passed through them.

After lunch we did a group exercise and watched a couple of films, one of which was quite hard-hitting, but before that I sat on a bench in the churchyard and had lunch with my uncle. My uncle hadn't brought sandwiches of his own, and I offered him one of mine, which had a Manchego, rocket and chutney filling.

'What's this? You need to get some proper food in you. You'll waste away. Look at you.'

'I'm fine.'

'It's all right, actually. Tasty. Thanks.'

Above the bench, the branches of an old yew tree shook slightly in the breeze. The door to the church was arched and wide and the texture of its old, worn oak resembled the scratches of a rabid animal. Back when I was young, my uncle was always climbing trees and I was always following him. One time my uncle climbed a log over a tree across a river, and I followed him and fell in. Sitting here, it occurred to me that in some ways this man, who I had not seen or truly thought about for many years and no longer knew, had in some strange way brought me to this exact point in my life: climbing trees for a living, and enduring a day of conference-room punishment for driving a car too fast. I had not driven my car very fast on the occasion I had been caught speeding, it was true, but I did sometimes drive it far faster than I should have done, and that needed to change. I had always liked going in my uncle's cars, because they were faster than my dad's. That part of me still existed, despite myself.

'Not surprised you didn't last in London, in that job. Knew it wasn't right for you. That's what you were like as a kid – always outdoors. You're better doing what you're doing now. There's a tree at my and Charlotte's place. Ash. Maybe you could look at it for us. It's got that disease.'

'Ash dieback.'

'Yep. That's it.'

'What exactly happened earlier?' I said.

'I don't know. I suppose the guy had written down the date wrong in his diary and wasn't supposed to teach today.'

'Maybe,' I said. 'I don't know.'

'People play pranks. My mate Paul did all the carpets in this place. You should look him up, if you need carpets.'

My uncle seemed reluctant to continue to discuss the big question of the morning, as if it was an emotional issue for him. My auntie Claire had said that was the problem with him: he wasn't up for discussing anything, or opening himself up emotionally. But it had ultimately been only one of the problems for them, a relatively minor part of why they hadn't stayed together.

We walked back to the hotel and as we sat down for the afternoon session, it occurred to me that the room was very much divided into two sets of drivers: those on the back two rows, who drove fast a lot of the time, were proud of it and would continue to do so after the course was over. And those of us on the front, who were embarrassed about being here, and would like to try to be better citizens. A couple of blokes on the back row heckled Matt when he claimed that speed cameras were of benefit to society and not a government scheme to generate easy revenue. My uncle probably would have been with them, had this been a few years earlier. Instead he lurked in a half-and-half area. Row three, leaning back a little, as if occupying some middle ground, not quite with anyone, sitting on the fence about his allegiances.

At the end of the day my uncle pointed out to me that we were now living remarkably close to each other, no more than four miles apart in this newish part of the country for both of us, but we did not arrange to meet again. By the time I said goodbye to my uncle in the car park, his face had changed: I had the sense that I was looking at him through a tunnel, and years and jowls had fallen off him every minute until he was physically the same man he'd been when I was younger. On his head was a strong shadow-memory of his thick, almost black hair, despite the fact that almost all of it had gone, the strands that remained being ever-weakened by heavy rain. The droplets slid down the church walls behind us and darkened the scratch marks on the door about ten yards from where, watching through the window, I'd lost sight of John, his walk just discernibly changing to a crawl as he disappeared from view. Within a year, my uncle was dead too. Not from a car accident, but cancer, although I never enquired as to which kind.

NINE TINY STORIES
ABOUT HOUSES

SEA HOUSE

The house leaned out over a corner of the sea almost as if the cliffs were a church wall and the house itself was a gargoyle stuck to the wall. When the couple reached their room, the first thing they noticed was a portrait of the devil hanging opposite the beds. The devil looked slick and smug in this illustration, like a man you were told to trust by someone who prized cleanliness above all other qualities, apart perhaps from the alleged quality of personal wealth. They would have been less scared if the devil had had red eyes and a pointier nose and a tail and looked more traditionally devil-like. While she applied her make-up, he turned the portrait so the devil faced the wall, then they went off to watch their friends get married.

She danced for several hours and he, joined by an

accomplice, harangued the DJ when the DJ ceased playing songs that people liked and began to play songs that he thought would make people impressed by his esoteric knowledge. By this point the bride's aunt had gone to bed and been woken again by a knock on the door of her room and opened it to find nobody there. By the time the couple got into bed they had drunk a lot of champagne. The room had two single beds and she seemed much further than three feet away from him in hers. 'Have you seen how round my bottom is?' she said, twisting her head to look back at it, as if for the first time, then fell asleep. He outlasted her only by a minute, the scarlet room spinning around him. He did not notice the three drawing pins in the bed and the other four stuck in his bare thighs until the next morning, when he was sober.

HOLIDAY HOUSE

She always remembered it as the best holiday house. Everyone had been there, the time she went. All the best people. There had been a big central room, a bit like a medieval banqueting hall, and the bedrooms were all off that, a perfect circle of them, with the exception of the crow's-nest bedroom, where her aunt and uncle slept.

She had been five and her parents were still together, and drove an orange VW Beetle. A wicker chair hung from the ceiling like the ones everyone had only previously seen in catalogues, and Pete sat in it and it crashed to the floor, which was surprising because everything about Pete was very skinny apart from his beard, which still probably didn't weigh all that much. All the cars outside smelled of their engines in a way cars didn't any more. She liked inhaling it.

These memories were so vivid and comforting that almost three decades later when she realised she lived near the house, she went to see it, and its new owners, who did not run it as a holiday home like their predecessors, very kindly showed her around. She wandered through the rooms, exclaiming at how small they all seemed compared to her memory of them. She thanked the current owners, thinking it best not to admit to them that she had got the wrong house.

RIVER HOUSE

Polly lived across the track from the house and Sam liked her a lot. Her main interests included dogs, books, cats, UFOs, fossils and bones. Before she'd left her husband, they had been burgled and he'd shown the police into the porch. The policeman had asked what was in the trunk in the porch and if anything had been taken from it. 'No, that's just my wife's bones in there,' he had replied. From her position across the track, with her small dog and large cat, Polly had watched the various tenants fall in love with the house then become derailed by life in eclectic ways. The river ran partly under the house and later, when Sam dreamed of the rooms, they were always very damp and overrun with swimming creatures that were oddly lizardlike and redolent of prehistory.

A few years after Sam left, Polly told him the details of the stabbing that happened in the house, which she said were different from those reported in the local media. She said she had taken a photo that Sam might want to see, which was of a ghost standing beside the gate to the field next to the house. The photograph wasn't a digital one, she said. She tried not to get involved with all that business. Sam said he'd like to see it and the two of them arranged to go for a walk a fortnight later, on the north coast, where she hoped to find dinosaur bones. A week later Sam received a phone call from Polly's daughter, informing him that Polly had died of an undetected brain tumour. During a digital clear-out half a decade later, Sam came across Polly's email address and a steamroller of sadness hit him: very different from the sadness he might have felt if he had stumbled across her physical address.

WOOD HOUSE

When I am in bed I hear the timbers on my house expand and crack. It's not an eerie crack, but I suppose it could be, one day, if somebody died in the house, and the house had some wisdom to impart about that. Nobody has died in the house so far. I am sure of it. Only Klaus and Rebecca lived in the house before me, and they are alive. I saw them just last week at the Lamb Feast in the village. The crack of my house sometimes wakes me up, but I never resent the disturbance. I listen to the house crack and then I stretch out in bed and hear the answering crack of my bones. It's an appropriate house to live in when your joints are beginning to decline. They don't just crack because I'm old, though. They cracked when I was young, too. I'd bend down in a bookshop to reach a novel on a low shelf and the ligaments in my knees would snap in an antisocial way, and if there were other people in the shop they'd turn around and wince. 'Oof, are you OK?' they'd sometimes ask, and I'd assure them that I was fine, that it didn't even hurt, not a bit, because it really didn't, and then I'd reach for the book I wanted, which was often about older people halfway across the world in wooden houses who lived lives that I wanted to understand and didn't but now do.

METAL HOUSE

I drove to the house for the first time in the billowy dark of a country night by the jagged steep coast and it felt like driving down a chasm into a place that belonged only to itself. The next morning, after waking everyone up by shouting in excitement at the sea in the way that only the natively landlocked do, I cooked three terrible eggs on an old electric oven, probably similar to the electric oven the band who'd recorded there in the seventies had cooked terrible eggs on. I was still wearing my coat at the time, having gone to bed with it on.

My dad had been in the band, but I never had known him, and I grew up avoiding his records. Now I listened to them a lot, but my mum didn't know that, and didn't need to. This weekend she thought I was in Banbury. She probably wouldn't check whether I was or not. Why would she? I was twenty-eight. Before bed there had been a collective scramble for firewood to make the big rooms warmer and I later remembered someone breaking an old chair and putting it on the fire but have realised this probably didn't happen and is in fact a memory of a scene from one of my favourite films, which has also made me question all sorts of things about memory, and by extension about history itself, which is often written by overimaginative people, and by wise people whose memories are failing.

An old wise person whose memory was probably failing and who hadn't been there anyway once wrote in a book that my dad broke down one of the doors of this house with an axe when he was under the influence of alcohol and hard drugs, but who was to say if that was true? I slept well in the house. I did not know if my bedroom was the one whose door my dad might or might not have broken down with an axe. It could have been. There was a one in six chance. The flagstone floor featured a carpet of dust and there were unpacked boxes everywhere, but the beds were perfectly made and the sheets felt expensive. The morning was cold as we drove back up the chasm, listening to the record made in the house, which from then on would always sound like cold and dust and terrible eggs to me, in the best way possible.

PROGRESSIVE HOUSE

As long as the electricity lasted, the house ran very smoothly and nobody got upset. Popular jargon was repeated, prompting a sound like laughter, and decisions were made by committee, without undue emotion. Nobody did anything unwise that they later regretted. Outside, the seasons continued their fade into each other until finally they were an indistinguishable whole.

MOOR HOUSE

We went to bed and about five minutes later we heard a loud slamming noise downstairs. I leapt from under the covers and ran downstairs to find the kitchen door open to the silent late summer night. I had checked the kitchen door was locked, even though we hadn't used that kitchen door; we had used the other kitchen door. This kitchen door had definitely been locked, with a key turned on the inside. Now it was open. What it opened on to was a garden, a sloping field of messy geriatric August wild flowers and moorland: a space of around half a mile before you reached the neighbour's house.

The next day the air in the garden was thick and sparkly. Swallows and house martins dived under the eaves. We decided not to stay a third night. I didn't tell my friend, who had been loaning the house to us, about the door. I felt it would have been somehow ungrateful. We didn't talk about it until years later. By that time she had left the house. She said it had been creeping her out; her boyfriend particularly didn't like the ghost of the old woman, dragging her leg along the upstairs corridor every night.

VANISHED HOUSE

After university Stephanie worked as an estate agent and it never felt right – not that she had ever expected it to. People thought being an estate agent made her a bad person, but what it actually made her was a person who was successfully paying off her student loan. She felt awful fleecing people – some of whom she grew to like – of cash, so she transferred from sales to lettings, until she realised that as a department this was arguably even more venal, with its intangible hidden fees, materialistic water-cooler car chat and dumbo snobbery. But she would always feel oddly grateful to the property world as, had she never been in it, she would never have recoiled from it in such a way that prompted her to boldly do something she had always really wanted to do, which was dye her hair blue and play the harp. Nobody paid her money for dyeing her hair blue, but eventually a small income began to emerge from her harp, which she played to old people and unwell people. She also sometimes walked over the back fields to the farm cottage where Mr Blackwood lived and played the harp for him, but she didn't charge for that.

One time Mr Blackwood, who was eighty-one, had to have stitches in his head after falling down the stairs. The stitches were blue. 'Look!' he said to Stephanie. 'Just like yours. Does that mean I am alternative now and can join your gang?'

It was fine carrying the harp over the fields to Mr Blackwood's but she wouldn't have liked to have to lug it any further than that. She rarely saw anyone else on the walk there or back. One day she was passing around a drumlin with a copse on top of it at the edge of one of the fields and was surprised to walk past a lady of about her age and height. They said hello to each other, shyly. The lady did not have blue hair or a harp, but her body language in greeting was similar to Stephanie's: the same half-smile, the same left-leaning dip of the head. As the day went on Stephanie became more and more aware of just what an uncanny resemblance the woman had to herself. 'I think I walked past me in a field earlier,' she joked to her friend Kazza in the pub that Friday.

Stephanie did take an interest in local history, but not a thorough or time-consuming one, so she didn't know that the field behind the drumlin had been the site of a farmhouse until around the time of the Civil War. For the last century that it stood, villagers had avoided going near the farmhouse because of a story about a woman who had shut her sister in the house and set fire to it after a fight over a man. They said that after the sister burned to death, her bones had been interred in the walls of the house when it had been rebuilt, the smaller ones arranged to form runes, and her voice screamed down the chimney in agony every night. Apotropaic scratches and patterns were found on lintels and door frames by future tenants. People were surprised that it had been the fair sister, not the dark sister, who failed to get the man, then did the murdering.

Some minor parts of the house's structure remained to this day, but they had been pressed deeper into the ground over the years by weather and the hooves of sheep and five or six horses. All you could see now was grass and dandelions and dog's mercury. In town a couple of the older folk in the less pretentious pubs remembered the story about the sisters, which they'd been told by their grandparents, with some details fabricated. It was still mentioned in a couple of the rowdier pubs, where you still heard accents, but there wasn't much of that kind of talk in town. It was a gentle place now. Stephanie knew the place had its drawbacks, but she had grown to like it more, partly for the very fact that she'd once gone away. It was just about right for her. It had a harp shop, but not a guitar shop, and she thought that said a lot about the kind of place it was.

PARTY HOUSE

The house looked extremely well kept and even sparkly in the estate agent's photos, but when we moved in we gradually began to realise how rampantly it had been enjoyed by the previous owners. We felt a little like people who had bought quite a high-grade second-hand car without realising its previous driver had been a boy racer. Except it wasn't just a car; it was our house. It was the main place we wanted to be, not just a machine we used to get to places we wanted to be.

The kitchen sink was choked with fat and when the plumber took the pipes apart we struggled not to retch at the smell. The door to the downstairs toilet fell off its hinges, almost crushing Judith Lawless when she visited with a stepladder and cake. I moved an old shelving unit in the garage, to replace it with my newer shelving unit, where I liked to keep my tools, and discovered that somebody had drawn a bulbous cock on the wall behind it, with some semen coming out of it, but not a lot. We both thought the cock looked tired, maybe from weeks of non-stop hedonism and overexertion. When we opened drawers and cupboards in the house, our hands often stuck to them. We began to picture gatherings of thirty or forty people where syrup was prevalent, if not mandatory.

In the garden, under a thin layer of fool's compost, we found a space hopper, dozens of bricks, five bags of sand, half an old rusty barbecue and a bike. It wasn't until a week or so in that we started finding the masks. We discovered seven in total, over the course of eleven years. We found them beneath the lining of drawers, in the crevices between kitchen units, behind the front panel of the boiler. One I found taped to the underside of the grate covering our septic tank when it got blocked and I had to open it up. It was soggy and faded, but I knew what it was. All the masks were the same: a black-and-white photocopied photograph of a man's face, with the eyeholes poked out. The man had floppy, confident, shoulder-length hair and was grinning, but, without the eyes to back it up, it wasn't a proper grin that you could trust.

We told ourselves stories about the night of the masks: the moment when the man, whose birthday it was, had returned to the room, and his friends had all put the masks on and sung 'Happy Birthday' to him. He'd had to pretend to enjoy it, but hadn't, at all. Later, when he'd passed out, his own eyeless face staring back down at him from the tallest leaves of an umbrella plant, the hiding had commenced, fuelled by a specific auxiliary creativity that comes only from drunkenness. Guests scattered to all points of the house. A couple who didn't know the man well took a couple of masks home and one surprised the other by entering their bathroom naked save for the mask, which turned out to be one of the small final straws in the decline of their relationship.

The man whose face was in the mask was an actor and I hadn't heard of him at the time, but when he died many years later I recognised his face, even with its new eyes. They were surprisingly bright eyes, despite the fact that the photo the newspaper had used was from a sad time when he had been caught drunk driving and briefly vilified for it on social media. I suppose that might have been all relative, though. Even sad eyes look bright compared to no eyes. Only a couple of years before that, I'd received a message from the people who bought the house from us to say they'd found another one of the masks in the loft. They asked if it was important and I said it was and requested that they send it to me at the address I'd given them for all mail and other future correspondence.

THE POOL

Here they come, the Lankester brothers, bouncing along the woodland path, and it's not like just any brothers you might see bouncing along a woodland path. It's a spectacle. Nobody's there to see it right at this moment, but it's still a spectacle. If you witnessed a squirrel stop what it was doing to gawk, it would be totally understandable and not a cause for questions. Spring happened, properly, finally, just today, after weeks of rain, and few humans have ever looked as correct in spring's rush as the Lankesters. Twenty and twenty-two. They seem a central part of the season's ruddy health. Celandines, wood anemones, and the Lankesters. As they follow the river's curve, their feet thump hard on tree roots and the very last of autumn's leaf mulch. There are casualties, inevitably. Over the course of a mile and a half, five oil beetles perish. A money spider flees the shadow of one of Simon's size-eleven trainers, only to run directly into Dylan's path. It was ailing, already two legs short of a full set, and would have died by nightfall anyway. You don't get abundant life like this without death. Any idiot knows that.

How many humans achieve a smoothly functioning body, of popularly desirable dimensions, in adulthood? If you researched the matter and looked at the hard data honestly, you might find it stark. But right now the Lankesters appear to have done as well as anyone in the big genetic shake-up. They are tall, but not above the height where tallness can become awkward. Other men have been known to stop in their tracks and stare, coveting their hair density. Their beard lines are consistent, unpatchy. Their complexions speak of Duke of Edinburgh awards and adventurous gap years and nutritional awareness. There is no sense that either of these boys – and they are still boys, despite what they believe – could ever become stooped or waylaid by a paunch. In the last year, Simon, the eldest, has just begun to suffer very slightly from irritable bowel syndrome and become afflicted more noticeably with his dad's crooked nose, but Dylan, an inch taller, when seen from a distance of anything more than a yard, appears to be a blemish-free and quirkless physical specimen. Looking at him, it's possible to believe he doesn't even have ancestors.

Both brothers really own rooms when they walk into them. They are not presently about to walk into a room; they are about to walk into a small clearing beside an inlet of the river, where a shelf of granite extends over the water, and the sun, while largely blocked by foliage, shines down fiercely on the rock through one shaft of space between the oaks. But they are about to own that too. Michael, a person with a tendency to really rent a corner of a room when he walks into it, is the first to hear the voices of the Lankesters and, though he joins in when Ella and Rach hear them too and Rach shouts, 'Yay! They're here!' and runs in their direction, his heart sinks a bit. For the last twenty minutes, he has had the girls' undivided attention. Ella has been sitting behind him on the rock shelf, her legs straddling him, grooming his neck, picking at invisible abrasions and pimples in a way that has been surprisingly pleasant. Rach has been a captive audience while he has described the plot of the film script he is writing. The film is about a gangland killing and she has listened intently, not voicing her main thought, which is that Michael is possibly the person she has met least likely to have any inside knowledge about a gangland killing.

'Oh my God. You would not fucking believe what just happened,' says Dylan, placing his bag and the camcorder on the ground.

'What?' says Rach.

'Seriously, man,' adds Simon. 'I don't think you want to know.'

'Come on – you can't say that then not carry on,' says Ella. She offers Simon an open bag of nuts. 'What happened? These are addictive. They've got this spicy jalapeño covering. Once you start, that it's. It's all over. You're fucked.'

'Shall I tell them?' says Dylan. 'No, you tell them. You saw the guy first. You were the one who filmed it.'

'OK,' says Simon. 'So Dylan already went in the river . . .'

'What?' says Ella. 'We haven't been in yet! We were waiting here patiently for you. That's not fair.'

'Not fair at all,' mumbles Michael into his espadrille. He is the kind of person who rarely feels listened to by the world, which has the effect of making his voice lower, compounding the problem. People are always finding bits of lint on his face and picking them off, just as he's telling them something that really matters to him.

'I just went in once,' says Dylan. 'It's no big deal. And it doesn't really count.'

'We went up Parsley Hill, the other way, down by Brick Kiln Lane,' says Simon. 'That's why we're late. I was just driving past there the other day and remembered those stairs that Johnno hammered into the tree trunk. Remember? About five years ago? No. You weren't here then. But you remember, Michael, right? Anyway, we walked up that way, and guess what, they're still there! So Dylan climbed up to the top branch, and I started filming it. You have to get the jump just right and hit this bit where it's really deep, otherwise you're buggered. Anyway, I'm still filming and then I spot something in the field on the other side of the river—'

'You will not fucking believe this, right.'

'Am I telling the story, or are you? So there's this field over there. You know? It's like this little nature-farm-type thing, and they have these weird sheep with massive horns that look like the bounty hunters in *Return of the Jedi*, and these tiny pigs. And, like about five or six goats, too, small ones.'

'Oh, goats are weird. I don't like their eyes.'

'Well, some people do. A lot. I mean, *really* a lot.'

'What are you on about?'

'So I'm filming Dylan in the water and then I see over in the field there's this goat, and there's this guy just sitting behind it. And I thought, "That's fucking weird. Why would you just sit behind a goat?" So I zoom in.'

'You would never fucking believe what he was doing.'

'What?'

'He was having a wank. Stretching the meat. Totally pulling himself off, right there.'

'Eeeeeugh.'

'So I carry on filming and it's like he's miles away, he's so into it that he's not even noticed us or heard the splash when Dylan landed in the water. And then after about a minute I see him look round in our direction and shit himself and then he puts his dick back in his trousers and starts running.'

'And you got all this on camera?'

'Yep. Do you want to see?'

'No. I'm not watching that.'

'I'll watch it.'

'What was the goat doing?'

'It was just eating grass or whatever, some stuff from the hedge. Just going about its business.'

'You need to go and tell the people there. Someone should call the police or something.'

'And tell them what? What could they do?'

'Here, have a look, anyway. You can hear me shouting, "Wanker!" at him as he runs off at the end.'

Above the five friends, the sun is reaching its maximum intensity for the day. Its rays reach the new leaves at the top of the ravine, then separate, then begin to re-form into a solid shaft as they hit the water, turning the jagged rocks deep beneath the surface to gold. It does not warm the pool much, and all five of them shout in happy pain as their heads re-emerge after their first jump. Ella is the most energetic, jumping again and again as the others spread out on the rocks, and as Rach observes Ella's height and her china-blue eyes and the neat way she stretches her arms above her as she leaps, she is reminded of the heron they disturbed earlier, further downstream: a creature with a touch of the spectre about it, something passing through dimensions, not supposed to be seen. When Ella hits the water she makes herself impossibly slight, and the impact is so quiet and smooth, it would not be a surprise if she did find another dimension down there to vanish into.

It is a delicious afternoon that will be rarer than any of them realise in future: a point where work is not intervening and they have the river to themselves. People pay vast sums of money to rent a lot less peace than this on a temporary basis. From here you can walk to the top of the ravine, then thrash through the new bracken for a mile, then reach a road, and if you did that right now, on this particular weekday afternoon, you would still not have seen another human. After that you could intercept the footpath running between the moor and the edge of town and you would still have not have found anyone. It would only be half a mile on from that that you would see the first other sign of two-legged life: a stooped man, fiftyish, hurrying back to his car, which he had parked in a diagonal, hurried way beside a clapper bridge. If you continued to follow him closely, you'd see him turn on the engine without fastening his seatbelt and the relief in his face as he pulled out and hit the tarmac, glad that he lived far away, glad in the knowledge that he would never be returning to these parts. But you'd see terrible fear too: of himself. He'd not been careful enough. Once before, he'd also not been careful enough, and he'd paid the price. The train line had been too close, and he hadn't bargained for the signal failure. He'd been too lost in it all to realise he was being watched. The argument for the defence had not stood up in court. No, the jury had not found it believable that you could be urinating in a field and a medium-sized farm animal could just 'happen' to unexpectedly back in to you. He had not enjoyed prison, had emerged from it grey and hollow-cheeked. He had told himself he would never be that careless again. There would be no touching in future. He had stuck to that, even when temptation overwhelmed him. But, still, he had not been careful enough. He had been lucky today, he hoped. He would not return here.

They feel indestructible, lazing on the rock in this heavenly light: Ella, Dylan and Simon, but also Rach and Michael, to a lesser extent. But none of them know it, because they have now felt indestructible for a couple of years at least, and a couple of years is a long time when you're young enough to feel indestructible. Ample time to get accustomed. Michael has waded across the river with the camcorder hoisted above his head and got some great footage of the other four in mid-flight. Dylan says he's had enough of a rest now and that he's going to go for the Big Daddy.

'What on earth is the Big Daddy?' says Rach, and he points to a small shelf of feldspar above them. 'You're not right, dude,' she says, as he begins to climb, ascending with tough bendy simian feet over sharp niggling rocks and ferns and thorns to the upper platform, made by some ancient land gods, just for him.

'Wait,' says Michael. 'I want to make sure I get this from the best angle.' And he wades to the opposite side of the ravine again with the camcorder and commences his own climb, only slightly less daredevil.

'OK,' says Dylan. 'Ready?'

'Ready!' says Michael, and he captures it all: the run-up, the leap through the shredded sunlight, the huge splash, the nervous wait for him to re-emerge.

'FFFFFFuuuuuucccckkkk!'

'Again?'

'Again.'

And he goes again, and again, five more times in total, each time making himself feel more alive, more Dylan,

Michael getting it all, but on the fifth time, maybe pushed by some small jealousy, wanting to be watched like Dylan is being watched, looking for a different angle, Michael steps a little far out and his foot slips. He grabs a root in the hillside as he falls, but to do so he must let go of the camera, which tumbles down the rocks. They all stare, somehow feeling that they can will it to catch on something and halt its descent, and the second and a half before it hits the water passes very slowly.

'You twat.'

'That cost four hundred quid.'

'It will be OK. It's waterproof anyway, right?'

Simon jumps into the water to look first, then Dylan, then Ella, then Simon again, then – scared, but pressed by guilt – Michael. But they have been particularly unlucky. In its descent, the camcorder has bumped down into a thin vertical corridor, too narrow for a human body, and wedged under an elbow of rock. It's darker in this part of the water, so impossible to see the camcorder's exact location from the point above, which appears to be the bottom of the pool. Above the ravine, the sun has moved around and no longer illuminates the river. It is evening, and spring is young, and the evenings have not yet lost their chill.

Nobody here knows it, but technology is on a historical precipice. In only two or three years, everyone will record everything. People will take devices much smaller than the one in the water to concerts and other live events and record experiences which, by doing so, they are simultaneously forgetting to have, then store them, never to be watched, on laptops and memory sticks. But right now making home recordings of your life is still a privilege, still feels a little special, and for Ella, Simon, Michael, Rach and Dylan, right now is the only context. The fact remains: there were some absolutely amazing jumps on there.

'There is no way I am just leaving it there,' says Simon. 'I'm so fucking coming back to get it tomorrow.'

Some days the warmth of the air feels like it is little to do with the sun at all. Today is not one of them. As they walk back down the path, the heat has been sucked from the gorge. Rach wonders aloud if it might be an idea for them to go to the farm and tell them what they saw. Simon says he might do that, but later. As Rach talks, her voice is stuttery with cold. Simon gives her his cardigan, but she continues to shiver, not unpleasantly, inhaling the parts of his odour that have clung to the dampish wool. As they come to a jerk in the river's knee, the sun performs an unexpected encore. Wood ants emerge and swarm in their thousands over dead bark at the side of the path, poised to squirt acid at anyone who makes the mistake of giving them any shit. A scarlet tiger-moth caterpillar basks on a dock leaf.

They turn up the bridleway towards the cars, along a bank of beech trees with mossy, exposed roots, and being in the dappled light under the new canopy feels like being in a bath of sorts. Bluebells are up. There is no sense of loss about the evening. Everyone will sleep deeply tonight, including a pygmy goat called Maxine who, in a field about half a mile away, is experiencing the most difficult part of her day, as she mistakenly begins to chew on part of an old polythene grain sack caught a hedgerow, then attempts to spit it out. Nothing else about life has fazed her recently. Her owners, Bob and Doris, are often telling people what a sweetheart she is. She likes people, is rarely bolshy around them, although there is a general consensus that some of her immediate contemporaries can be right bastards, if you catch them on the wrong day.

Summer does not live up to the promise of late spring. In July, it rains for twenty-one days in a row. Slugs are out in force on the garden walls of the cottage at the bridge. Almost nobody makes the effort to swim in the pool. In August a lone canoeist turns off the river's main artery and lets himself drift in lazy circles in the pool's centre. He thinks about everything he regrets and whether it was a mistake to choose the side of his second wife, as opposed to his daughter, during their dispute. He wonders, for the first time in years, about an animal he hit on a road outside Shaftesbury on a business trip, and whether it was a fox, or somebody's dog. Below him, the water is oil-black.

On one of the days that dance the line between summer and autumn, Lacey and Ray come to swim in the pool. They're staying in one of a group of six guest cottages in some farmland half an hour south of here, but he doesn't like the chlorine in the indoor pool there. He remembered an old college lecturer telling him about a dark, deep, tranquil space off the river and he is pleased to find it, using just an OS map and a decade-old memory. It's breezy and the surface is covered in leaves and they shout with joy as they splash about. But on the way back up the hill they are silent. He is poised to tell her a couple of things but he stops, thinking she will not be interested. He is suddenly conscious of how much she sighs in his company. He realises it has all been gone for her since this time last year.

In the winters the pool almost never freezes, but in heavy rain torrents of spume race over the rocks, and because of the angles, a kind of riptide is formed. Swimmers still feel it in summer, when the current is less ferocious, the water buffeting you two ways at once. It's like being inside a dizzy space where gravity has gone backwards and it gets a little more pronounced every year. There are injuries: sharp cuts on feet and ankles, mostly. Usually swimmers don't notice them until later. One leaper feels a twinge in his calf and looks to see blood streaming down it and a scratch that could be perceived as a large double toothmark. Some of the swimmers take a shortcut back to their cars afterwards, up the gorge, fighting their way through drying bracken and heather. Their cuts and scratches from this mix with the cuts and scratches from the pool and they can't any longer tell which are which. The bracken goes rust-coloured in autumn and in the strong winds of November the pool's surface gets seasoned with dry oak leaves that become soggy and decompose in no time at all.

One biting January day, a line of large crows perch on the higher rock shelf, which the bravest swimmers like to leap from. It looks like they're about to dive in formation but they don't. Down below, despite the eddies and all the changes in temperature, the camcorder looks exactly the same and the memory card, were it to be retrieved, would still be watchable. It is all still there. Gadgets like this are more resilient than folks realise. Silt has built up around the camcorder, wedging it more firmly in place. If you looked at the people on the film last year, you'd have thought of them as people from now, but just this year, they have started to look like people from an era that has passed. That is because it has been a decade since the film was made, and a decade is the exact amount of time it takes for clothing styles and attitudes to become palpably old. It is part of the reason why decades were invented.

In March of the following year, Maxine the goat dies after an uncomfortable period suffering from yolk boils on the neck, which is a disease also sometimes known as cheese mouth among goat people. It is agreed by Bob and Doris that she has had a good life.

Thick-skinned, incurious people who walk the narrow footpath above the rock shelf or swim in the water don't notice anything unique or ominous about the atmosphere in the pool, but a few more sensitive and intuitive souls remark on it. They see it like people who are able to see a quietness as an image. Something feels locked in, as if air has walls. But it's still part of a much larger place people are drawn to because of lightness and beauty. Some of the atmosphere is dispersed and absorbed into that, like piss in the sea.

Jane and Moon and Anya live for a summer in their van up in a layby on the byroad and often come down here with books and picnics and, as autumn edges in, to hunt for mushrooms. Moon comes down on his own some mornings and meditates. It only lasts ten minutes, but he would not be the same person facing the day the same way without it. Some days he feels, with his eyes closed, that the river is becoming part of him, rushing through him, coldly but not malevolently. One day, though, something else goes through him. It is not watery. The top of it is hard, double-spiked, and it pushes through his chest. When he opens his eyes he is no longer sitting. He is on his side, on the rock, and the sky is tilted. He stays motionless for some time.

Bill and Ian walk along the footpath above the pool. They are both fifty-four now, but since university they have done this every September, gone away for a week of hiking and drinking together, with the exception of one year, when Bill was recovering from Hodgkin's lymphoma. The trip is a tradition, and whoever else is in their lives at the time had bloody well better deal with it. Bill once locked Ian in a cupboard at their halls of residence for seven hours and has always mocked Ian for various facets of his appearance and his lack of sense in the areas of money and women. It is perceived as part of the jocular dynamic of their relationship. As they pass above the pool, Bill jokes about Ian's recent weight gain.

'You know what, mate?' says Ian. 'You're a cunt.

Always have been, and always will be.'

They continue the walk in silence. When Ian, who knows how much Bill loves rare fungi, spots an octopus stinkhorn beginning to erupt from a suberumpent egg beside the footpath, he doesn't say a word. Back at the B & B, they go straight to their rooms. They leave separately, early the next morning, without exchanging goodbyes.

Later in autumn, there are mists over the pool early in the morning, but nobody is there to appreciate them at their apex. The day's smattering of walkers arrives a little later. Belinda produces a tub of assorted nuts from her backpack and offers them to Karen, who declines. Karen feels a rage percolating inside her. She is overwhelmed with how shitting annoying it is that Belinda always has these nuts, and that she never stops eating them. If it's not nuts, it's dried fruit or spicy peas. There's always something. Karen suppresses bringing it up and making it an issue, but it takes all her energy. Her nails make deep red marks in her thighs, which will still be there tomorrow. By the time they have reached the knee bend in the river, she is calm. She asks Belinda about how Georgie is doing with her counselling. Karen tells Belinda she mustn't blame herself in any way. In the early hours of the morning a stray cat stalks the bank, a once-adored Birman called

Zara. After being driven out of her house by her owner's new Great Dane pup, she has wandered for three days and ended up down here after chasing a rabbit along the open moor above the gorge. It is a surreal and absurd place to be a stray cat and, as if in realisation of this, Zara turns in the opposite direction, sensing her way towards the cottage at the bridge, stopping every so often to rub the scent glands on the inside of her lip on thick stalks of heather and the low branches of blackthorn.

There is a line where mist becomes fog and during the early days of December it is crossed. But it's not during fog that what has been growing in the river breaks the surface and takes a look around. It's on a clear night after a frosty day where sheer cold has made resilient leaves surrender and quiver to the ground. Moonlight illuminates the shape so its horned shadow flickers on the rock wall behind it. Its only large witness is a roe deer on the bank above, which scarpers through the bracken, away from the river. But the shape isn't interested in deer and has not yet grown eyes to see them. That moment when it broke from water to air might have resembled a birth of sorts, but it wasn't really. It's already been here for a while and there's a long way to go yet: so much time, and all the strength that time gives. It's back in the water in moments and the calls of owls and the rush of water over ancient rocks and the rest of the undersong of the river night play on. Soon the year will turn over and not all that long after that, the swimmers will come again. A few more this time, thanks to technology's grapevine. They'll film and photograph themselves jumping off the rocks and as they leave they'll be keen to be home, feeling an excitement about the prospect of sharing the experiences and the ease with which they can do so. *Take me back*, they'll write beneath their photographs, only hours later.

ROBOT

One day I was hiking through a sharp cleft in the woods when I met a robot walking towards me up the sunken green lane. This was a surprise, because I'd been told that this particular part of the woods, where the nearest building was a mile away and the light was gauzy and filled with the duplicitous shadows of newly denuded branches, was a place where you might find piskies or faeries or maybe huge liminal dogs, but at no point had anyone mentioned the possibility of robots.

I say the robot walked towards me, but that is technically incorrect; it was more that he slid, on something between skis and metal feet. He bumped slightly over the exposed roots of beech trees, but took it in his stride, never appeared in danger of falling, until he was a foot from my face. He said nothing from his wide oblong mouth, so I took it on myself to be the one to begin the conversation.

'Where are you from?' I asked.

'The future,' said the robot.

'Which part?' I asked.

'A very distant part. Hard for you to imagine. Don't even try.'

'But are you not in danger of changing the course of history, now that you are here? You have already walked at least a hundred yards along this holloway. I know it's autumn, but there are still beetles and other insects on the ground. You've probably killed some of them with your feet. Everyone knows that can do irreparable damage to future events.'

'We have that figured out in the future. We have ways of sorting it. You really don't need to worry about that. People and robots have been time travelling for a long time in the part of the future where I come from. We have worked a lot of stuff out. Also, they're not feet. They're called rotorsocks.'

'Sorry.'

A strong gust of wind harassed the tops of the trees, and a few acorns detached from the branches and became a form of boisterous dry rain, almost hitting the robot and me.

'Would you like to see it?'

'See what?'

'The future.'

It was a vast question: probably the vastest I'd ever faced. 'Why not,' I concluded.

I had lost my job the previous month. This being only four months after my aunt, the one human being in the world I'd been genuinely close to, had been crushed to death in a tractor accident on the farm where she had lived and toiled. In all honesty, I was feeling quite gung-ho and nothing-to-lose about the point life had brought me to, so when the robot slid open a metal plate in his chest cavity and invited me to step inside, I did so with little hesitation. He was a much taller, wider robot than I'd realised, when I'd first seen him bumpsliding up the holloway on his rotorsocks, and I was able to climb inside his rib cage with little trouble, although it did help that I had become very thin of late, particularly since losing my aunt and my job.

There were some clanking, rusty sounds, like gears grinding, sounds far more clanking and rusty than I would have imagined might emerge from a robot devised in the very distant future, as opposed to merely the future. Then I felt a sensation that reminded me of the time I crossed the Channel from Dover to France on a hovercraft, except exaggerated a hundredfold, and more redolent of spinning than forward motion. This lasted what I took for about five minutes, but what you probably couldn't put a time length on in this limbo state between centuries (or was it whole millenniums?).

After that all was very silent, silent in a blanker, more bottomless way than even the woods when I walked in them at 3 a.m., searching for something I could not name, and while I'd been dimly aware of metal in front of me before, now it was too dark to see anything at all. I reached to touch the back of the robot's chest cavity, to give myself some spatial awareness, but I could feel nothing. I am still in this deep, silent blackness, writing this now, except I don't have a pen, and when I reached out with what I thought was one of my hands to touch my other hand, it wasn't there. One hand might still be there, but I cannot find another part of my body to use to check and make sure. There is absolutely no way of telling. I cannot feel anything of myself, in fact, physically, but I am still having these thoughts and recording them for posterity. I do not know where the robot has gone.

JUST GOOD FRIENDS

The illusion of an excess of choice had ruined modern romance. This is what, after three years in a cycle of being seduced by that excess of choice, recoiling at the ice-cold lie of of it, then being seduced by it again, Helen had concluded.

'But everyone goes online now,' Helen's friend Donna Rooney had said. 'It's just a fact of life. It's so hard to meet people these days.'

Donna was one of the fortunate ones: Mark had been only the second man she'd met romantically via the internet, the pair's intertwined needs had immediately appeared simple and compatible and there had never been any sense of either of them keeping the other in any kind of holding pattern while they waited to see if anything better came along. Also, Donna's statement, Helen felt, was a commonly spoken misinterpretation: seeking romance in a virtual environment wasn't an alternative or replacement; it was an *extra* way to meet people. The real world hadn't vanished; it was still there, with its pubs and evening classes and museums and friends of work colleagues and dance floors and attractive strangers eating apples on park benches.

When you first looked at a dating app or website, even when you'd narrowed your focus down to those of an appealing social demographic or appearance or age group, the excitement was that of being presented with a large train entirely full of available people. It was only later that you realised just how crowded with other available people the carriages on that train were, all jostling for the attention of the available people you liked, loudly eating crisps, wiping their greasy fingers on the upholstery and pushing their way down the aisles, sometimes, in the process, knocking you off balance so you fell backwards onto the emergency buzzer.

It had recently occurred to Helen that she no longer wanted to be part of that jostling and, more to the point, would be better matched in the long term to a person who was also not part of it. Someone who had not had their brain reconditioned by it. Shopping for love, she had noticed, seemed to put people in an accelerated, attention-deficit headspace. Conversations were quickly forgotten, names, even. A tall and photographically imposing person who entered rooms with surprising deftness, Helen had returned from the toilet towards the end of another nonplussing encounter, unnoticed by her companion for the evening, a fellow academic named Brian or Steve or Carl, to spot, via a gap between his right shoulder and ear, that he was already back on the app through which they had met, scrolling towards his next target. She could not find it in herself to be incensed, having often done the same herself, although to her credit she did always wait until she had at least boarded the train home. That was the internet all over, though. 'This has been a disappointing life experience. But do not worry. Look what I have for you next!' it told you, without end.

It was in the spirit of a greater slowing down, as well as a new philosophy about romance, that in March of her thirty-fifth year Helen removed the SIM card from her smartphone, transferred it to a clamshell model of almost a decade's vintage, and set off to the opposite side of the city for the first of ten evenings of Buddhist meditation. January had been frittered in a series of intense but counterproductive conversations with an IT consultant called Jamie who, despite clicking 'like' on all of Helen's last seventeen photographs, showed no inclination to set a date to meet in the flesh. February had been sucked away with worry about her mum's surgery. It was only a few hundred years ago, in pre-Gregorian times, that the new year began in March, and that made a lot of sense to Helen today. Years were real and legislated expressly by nature, but months were just stories we told ourselves to give our lives structure. On the street where Helen lived – a line of Victorian terraces petering out into a patch of messy almost-countryside, blemished with rotting machinery and aloof horses – it felt like spring was finally sprinkling its colours over an invisible wall, and this struck her as a far more logical point for a year to begin. The new season seemed to follow Helen through the door of the Sweetland Meditation And Yoga Centre, where the walls were green and lilac and two nonthreatening crew-cutted men sat on a worn sofa sipping peppermint tea: thin, light people, leaflike in their aura.

It became very apparent, after only minutes of her first session, that Helen was not immediately sexually attracted to any one of the other sixteen people in the room, and she silently reprimanded herself for the disappointment she felt at this realisation. This was not what her March new year's resolution was about: it was about prioritising her own passions, putting herself in good places, throwing herself into activities that interested her. Besides, as she was reminded by her teacher, Preminand, the space she was in was one where goals were not important. There was no 'correct' way to meditate, she was told. She suspected that this must be at least partly untrue, since surely if someone was here in the room fighting or playing table tennis, that would be the opposite of the correct way to meditate. But even if she was not getting her breathing exercises totally right, or totally succeeding in blocking out thoughts of unreturned emails and job lists, it was a relief to be forced to just sit still on a cushion by someone for a couple of hours and do nothing: a task that should have been achievable at home but always ended up befuddlingly beyond her reach.

On the way home her new state of stillness and calm was such that the voice of the narrator of the audiobook in her earphones seemed to be running at double speed. Turning into the avenue, she was aware of colours in the dark: new petal shapes, front-door aesthetics. A dark blue Japanese off-road vehicle she often saw parked at the end of the road was not here and she appreciated the texture of the gravel in the space where it normally sat. A pile of lentils had been spilled on the pavement. Two cats – Mitsky, who lived with Deborah and John from number 14, and another, fatter one she thought of as Ginger Ron – sat together on the wall opposite her house in a silence that suggested they'd been disturbed mid-gossip.

After the third of the weekly sessions, a girl called Andrea with perfect posture and a nest of unapologetic hair said she was meeting a friend at the Horse and Star and anyone else who fancied a drink was welcome to join them. Five meditators, including Helen, took her up on the suggestion. The pub was just the sort Helen liked: nicely dingy, slight suspicion of woodworm, jukebox, no shiny black vinyl chairs or gastro menus boasting of tautological pan-fried meals. The seven of them commandeered two four-seater benches either side of a long, pockmarked, coffin-shaped table. Behind them, teenagers just slightly too complicatedly dressed to be goth fell laughing through the door leading to the crypt beneath the bar at intervals of around a minute, allowing half-grumbles of subterranean local punk rock to waft into the room.

The conversation turned to Buddhist practices as alternative to therapy, and Helen attempted to bring Peter, a quiet man perched next to her, into the fold, but instead drifted into her own separate discourse with him. Helen had arrived late for that evening's session and, seeing her searching in vain for a cushion to perch on, Peter had been kind enough to fetch one from the store cupboard. Now they spoke of the *metta bhavana*, the 'loving kindness' meditation they'd been introduced to earlier in the evening, in which they were asked to bring more and more people into their heart. Helen admitted it had got a little out of control in the end, as she'd found all sorts of unexpected people and animals arriving in her heart, including her postman, a cow, three neighbourhood foxes and a stoat she'd seen last year on holiday on the Gower Peninsula. Everyone had then split into pairs to talk about a person in their life they felt a particular love for, and why. Helen told Peter she had talked about her mum: her unfussy strength, her lack of self-pity, especially after her recent operation. Peter did not say who he had talked about with his partner.

'How is your mum now?' asked Peter.

'She's doing well,' said Helen. 'She is made of something tougher than me. Something a bit leathery.'

'I'm really glad to hear that.'

Jet-black-haired and a little haunted around the eyes, Peter had a strong, large nose, but was otherwise delicate-featured, and arranged himself like a man keen to hide his tallness. It was only when she saw him stand to go to the bar and order more drinks for the two of them – a lemonade for him and a strong wheat beer for her – that she got a sense of his full height. She noticed that he would periodically stroke the table, paying it close attention. He told her it was oak, felled at least forty years ago. He asked her about her job. He told her that he'd heard that the museum where she worked was very nice, but had not had chance to visit himself. Each time she attempted to ask him a little about himself, he had a very skilled way of diverting the conversation back to her.

Outside, the Fens had brewed up one of their thin mean winds then faxed it east, where it zipped down the alleys and streets of the city. A tiny woman from the course who seemed to have been hugely enjoying her own body all evening, running her hands across her arms and chest at regular intervals, instigated a session of goodbye hugging. Helen wrapped her arms briefly and awkwardly around Peter and wondered precisely where in his jacket he resided.

The weekend was much warmer and Helen headed to her favourite spot near the river with a book. Three men in wetsuits swam smoothly with the current, like big pacifist leeches, and tantalising snatches of conversation from passing walkers blended not unappealingly with experimental prose.

'No way is that a real dragon. I've already seen five.'

'Good old Johnny Two Dicks. Always there when you need him.'

'So that's her uncle, right? The one who saw Mandelson at the gym. He has no respect for boundaries.'

'Is it good?'

It took Helen a moment to register that the last sentence was directed at her. She turned to see Peter standing behind her, looking no more evident in a shirt than he had in his coat the other evening.

'It's quite trippy. That might be something to do with the fact that it's translated from Japanese. I don't know. Or maybe it would be even more trippy if you read the original Japanese version. I'm finding it slow-going.'

'I'm a really slow reader. I tend to still read a lot of stuff I loved as a kid.'

'Nothing wrong with that.'

They walked back in the direction of the city, keeping to the river most of the way. Peter stopped to help two men carry a large canoe out of the water and Helen was surprised at how little exertion he displayed in doing so. She asked him what his plans were. He said he had just fancied a walk in the sun, and had no particular destination in mind. Helen said she'd wondered about catching a film later at the Picturehouse but was playing her afternoon similarly by ear. Peter asked her a little more about her job at the museum. It was closed today for refurbishment, but there was no actual work going on and Helen said she could open up and show him around if he liked.

'So it's your job to categorise stuff when it arrives?' he asked, as Helen unlocked the museum's archive area.

'That, and various other stuff. Payroll. Interviews, sometimes. There aren't enough of us working here that everyone can settle to just one role. A lot of what I do is about rejection. People don't realise how many donations we receive that are totally worthless or irrelevant. I spend a lot of time gently letting people down.'

Helen showed Peter some of the more interesting recent arrivals: two Victorian eel traps, a hammered dulcimer made by a local craftsman, and a writing desk that had originally been used by a student in the university halls in the late seventeenth century. Whenever a curio was made out of wood, Helen noticed that Peter inspected it particularly carefully, taking time to appreciate its joins and grain. At the pub afterwards, he asked her about her mum's recovery again, and about the life-sculpture class she had started: another of the resolutions of her deferred new year. His flair for filing away small pieces of personal information for later was as impressive and generous as his selfless conversationalism. He drank two lemonades and she drank two pints of strong dark ale from a local craft brewery. The ale made her more talkative and all this left her with the feeling of having monopolised the evening. Outside, in another small unexpected Fenland breeze, Peter struggled to make the zip on his jacket – an anorak, not the bomber from the other day – click into place and she assisted, feeling more like a mum than she had felt within living memory. As she solved the problem, he stood patient and still and trusting.

Helen had spent time alone in the company of plenty of ethereal men before. A couple of years ago she had dated a musician who had played lute at a folk-classical concert held at the museum. The musician spoke sparingly and when he did it was largely in his own whispered lexicon of Beat literature references and angular observations about cloud formations and the Milky Way. To Helen this, initially, was intriguing in the way an overheard conversation in a foreign language can be intriguing but later came the realisation not dissimilar to the one that you might have about the same overheard conversation in a foreign language, upon having it translated for you and finding out that it was really just about that week's shopping list, or somebody's marginally painful foot blister.

The musician was well read in a posturing, self-conscious way, a little lazy, and had a surprising lack of emotional depth, especially for someone who found so much of it with an instrument in his hands. Peter was different. His ethereality had no posturing to it and she never hit an emotional wall when talking to him. As he turned the conversation again and again back to her, she saw a listening softness in his eyes, and found herself telling him more and more: about work, about her mum, even about some of her romantic disappointments. After dates with so many men who had been so keen to have their opinions heard, their stories laughed at, she enjoyed this contrast, but after their fifth evening together in as many weeks, it occurred to her how truly little she knew about him. One fact was that he worked 'with wood'.

'You mean carpentry?' she asked.

'Sort of,' said Peter.

He had very nice hands: long-fingered without being bony. Hands you'd be very unlikely to find on a building site but which might craft something unique and memorable out of timber. A big contrast to her last but one boyfriend, Richard, who grew potatoes, and had hands that were all palm, deep and thick; such a contrast, so exotic, that when she first touched one of Peter's hands, she held on to it for an awkwardly long time. This was on their fourth date (were these dates? she still wasn't sure), when he walked her home past the dark blue Japanese off-road vehicle and the last of the spilled lentils and Ginger Ron the cat on his wall, then, by way of farewell, offered the most gentle of handshakes. By the beginning of June, a serene time of the year, slowed by the effects of a full ten weeks of breathing exercises and mindfulness, Peter and Helen had seen each other – outside the confines of the meditation course – nine times. In those encounters, he had not once come close to kissing her.

Something intangible, in rivalry to the draw of his gentle, sweet face and artist's hands, had made her hold back too, despite not being much of a holder-back, on the whole. Nonetheless, when she took off to spend four days with her mum on the west coast, she felt the need to give him notice about it, in a manner that you might not quite feel the need to do with someone who was just a friend.

Big sheets of black rolled in from the Atlantic, casting shadows over the water and the orthodontic pewter cliffs, then quickly got changed and replaced with cleaner, brighter sheets. Alice led the way, charging up and down the steep natural staircases in the rock, bellowing greetings to a party of passing surfers who were carrying their boards to the beach. Helen's mum was a little thinner, a little greyer around the eyes, but if you overlooked that, it was as if the tough winter had never happened. Helen struggled to keep up. This walk, which they had done before, always felt a little like being inside a washer-dryer for its full cycle; a budget model, whose drying function was slightly suspect. June was different here: there were hailstones, but also fierce sun and warm salt wind.

'So he's not really *said* he's your boyfriend?'

'He's not said much. He just listens to me and wants to walk everywhere. And I mean everywhere.'

'Well, he sounds just delicious. If only I could find a beautiful tall man who wanted to hear what I have to say.'

Alice had actually dated too, until a couple of years ago. When you were sixty-three, you expected plenty of baggage, but all too often, even on top of that, you found an extra storage room out the back for left luggage. The fantasist with the fake military career and the secret wife. The con man with the prison record. Helen did not ask Alice about her more recent love life. The main thing was that she seemed well, and, despite its lack of romantic prospects, life overlooking this serrated headland suited her. She had moved to a city just after Helen left home and felt out of place, like a strand of lichen blowing around a smoky pool hall, then moved back. Alice's current house felt as much like home to Helen as anywhere, even though it had never been home. Reaching the top of the cliff, the two of them could just make out the rooftops of the village where they'd both lived until Helen was six, much of that time with Helen's dad. The house over there was just smudgy memories now, memories of memories: the stepping stones over the small creek to the rear, a model of the village that Helen's dad had made for her from papier mâché, the old empty cottage up the hill with its thick, knobbled walls, a well she'd been obsessively warned by Alice not to venture close to on small solo adventures, which Alice encouraged. Alice told Helen she'd been a child boundlessly happy in her own company; the last of a generation who still went to the woods alone. But Helen had only the dimmest recollection of that version of herself. Her abiding memory of childhood was at school in the town, inland from there: roles in plays, countless friends, the excitement of the day everyone arrived at school and found games painted on the concrete playground in bright colours. Had there been a maypole, or was that historical transference: a children's TV show she was thinking of from the time? No. There was actually a maypole.

Before Alice and Helen turned inland across a field, unusually boggy for June, a dog emerged from a farm and joined them. Helen didn't know what kind of dog it was. She assumed it was one of those ones that are just a dog. After a mile, the dog transferred to another party coming the other way, a man in a black cagoule and a woman in a red cagoule. Almost all the walking couples here wore gender-specific anoraks of this combination. They'd almost reached an isolated hilltop church and a lone black figure walked the washed-out path to it, creating a scene that appeared monochrome even though it wasn't. Dusk had calmed the weather: there were no more black sheets arriving from the sky above the water.

Alice admitted she'd been worried about Helen earlier in the year. Alice had been worried about *her*? Yes. She had not seemed herself, not very present. It was true that Helen now barely recognised her winter self: it was as foreign to her as Alice's, on that hospital bed. Her view of breakdowns had been very different when she was younger: a vision of a person physically collapsing, making undignified noises, surrounded by tissues. But it was perhaps possible to have a breakdown without actually knowing it, due to the way time had fortified you to cope with it. Helen felt a lack of answers in her life but was much more centred now; a feeling of panic at the edge of everything had gone. On top of that, this place made her another, different person. It was the air, which was full of risk, but more alive than the air where she lived. But the chilly nights took you unaware; the wind that was trapped by the steep hills didn't jab at your ribs like an early spring Fenland wind, but it still got in the big old houses beyond the cliffs on the colder summer nights. When they got home Alice lit a fire and thrashed Helen at Scrabble, like always.

Back in the city, Helen left a couple of messages for Peter but received no response, via voice or text. On Tuesday a man with a beard so thick it gave a slight impression that he was just some eyes and a mouth visited the museum and, upon leaving, asked Helen for directions to a gallery in the centre of town. As she began to give them, the man rootled around for a pen in an overfull parka coat pocket. She noticed that one of the objects he pulled out of the pocket was a smartphone, which made her wonder why he hadn't just looked up the gallery on that, but she was too polite to point it out. He also pulled out a large, smooth stone with a hole in the centre. 'Nice hagstone,' said Helen.

Three hours later, just before the museum closed, when Helen was moving an old bawdy pub sign from an alcohol-themed display to storage, the man returned, shyly handed her a folded slip of lined notepaper, and left. Marge, who was working on reception, was around, so Helen didn't open the piece of paper until ten minutes later, when she was in the toilet.

You are very beautiful, it read. *But I don't like to put people on the spot or invade their space. So please feel free to tear this up and never think of it again. But if you would be amenable to it, I'd very much like to buy you a drink. Rob.* Beneath this a telephone number was written.

On Wednesday, Helen arrived home to find Peter leaning against the wall, waiting for her. He looked greyer than usual, darkened in the joins of his face. His hands were hidden deep inside his coat sleeves, giving him the appearance of a brittle plant you might wrap in old cloth to protect it from a hard frost.

'Hi. I've been worried about you. I tried to call, lots of times.'

'I'm sorry. I thought you might have. I've not been well. And I've got a problem with my phone company. I hoped you'd be home on time today. But I would have waited. It's a nice day.'

'What kind of not well?'

'I don't know. I think I ate things.'

She invited him in and, for the first time, he accepted. She offered him a tour of the house and he surveyed the rooms blankly, uncritically. Then they stepped out into the garden, where Tania was playing on the rope swing. The rope swing had been attached to an ash tree by the house's previous owners and was in the rear of the garden, where there was a gap in the fence, leading to next door, where Tania, who was seven, lived with her parents, Nick and Zoe. Helen liked Nick and Zoe, so had not felt any pressing need to repair the gap in the fence. Tania often came through it to play on the swing, and to tell Helen about the book she was writing, which she said was about an owl who was friends with a fridge. She introduced Tania to Peter but, in an unusually sullen mood, Tania didn't say hello, and gave him a long, sceptical stare. Helen sensed in Peter a keenness to be back indoors.

Helen did not have a lot of food in, but managed to cobble together a curry for Peter and herself from some green beans, potatoes and cauliflower. He sat apologetically on the corner of an armchair, with the plate on his knee, and picked at the meal like an endangered bird, nervous of impending extinction.

'How was Cornwall?'

'Wet, but good.'

'I like that bit.'

'Which bit?'

'Well, all of it. It's nice.'

'Have you been off work?'

'Yes. But I didn't have many jobs this week, so it was OK. I don't like work.'

'Who does, I suppose? It's like nothing when we're young prepares us for how much time it is sucking away from our lives. I can't complain. My job isn't all that taxing most of the time.'

'Mmmm,' said Peter, noncommittal.

Helen poured a glass of red wine and offered one to Peter, purely out of politeness. He surprised her by accepting, then draining the glass in one, while pulling a wincing, vinegary face. She poured him another, smaller one and he did the same. He had told her he liked jazz, or maybe he hadn't told her that, but she did remember that when they'd been in a café in the city centre the other week, he'd seemed to perk up and tune in when Jimmy Smith's version of the *Peter & the Wolf* soundtrack had come on. Now she chose a Milt Jackson live album from 1965, nothing too far out. Peter didn't seem to notice it. He really did look unwell.

'Are you OK?'

'Fine.' At this precise moment the doorbell rang and Peter sprang up, immediately losing his balance and crashing into the sideboard then tripping on his own tangled legs and hitting the floor, twisting awkwardly at the ankle as he did.

'Oh my God! Are you hurt?'

'No,' slurred Peter. 'I don't know.'

Reluctantly, Helen left him on the floor and went to find out who was at the door. It was Rebecca, who had some flyers for her new local history class, which she was wondering if she could give to Helen to take to the museum and leave in the foyer. Helen didn't extend an invite to step beyond the threshold to Rebecca, a caring person who could not resist finding a degree of entertainment in the problems of others. Back when Helen felt beset by romantic frustration, at the end of last year, Rebecca had often lent an ear but had soon begun to make Helen feel like a walking soap opera. Helen had withdrawn from Rebecca as a friend since then, just as she now withdrew back into the house, alone: slowly, with as little drama as possible. It took around six minutes in total and in that time Peter had fallen into what appeared to be a deep sleep on the floor. He looked very peaceful, although his legs retained some of the ungainly twist of his descent. She gently rocked his shoulder and he half opened his eyes, mumbled. Nothing intelligible. One word sounded a little like 'lost', but Helen couldn't be sure.

She managed to return Peter to an upright position and encouraged him to ascend the stairs in a half-crawling way, offering a shoulder for support. She led him into her bedroom and he face-planted into the mattress, which made it difficult for her to get the duvet over him. She had experience of men using drunkenness or feigned drunkenness as a ploy to try to stay the night, but she felt sure that was not the case here, even though she was equally sure Peter couldn't be *that* drunk. After all, he had only had a glass and a half of wine. She returned to the living room, checked some emails, drank another glass of wine, watched the second half of a film she'd started watching the other day, a dank tale of a psychotic preacher stalking children through a noir landscape.

She went back to check on Peter twice during this time and he was comatose but breathing steadily. Despite her having lived here for almost nine months, the spare bedroom remained a small city of unpacked boxes, and the fairly high-grade airbed she owned was trapped behind several of them. She didn't much fancy sleeping on the sofa, so at around 11 p.m. she crept under the covers beside Peter, sticking to her usual side of the bed, but maybe a little more so than usual. He did not stir.

Helen dreamed that Tania was on the rope swing again and Helen was watching her, annoyed at not being able to have a go. But when she finally took over she realised that the rope swing wasn't here in the city, it was in a much more rural place. As she swung higher, she could just about see the stepping stones behind the house on the coast where she used to live with her mum. The rope swing was getting really high now, and spiky branches prodded her head and it began to bleed, but she kept going higher, in an attempt to get a better view of the stones, even though the blood was running down her forehead beginning to get into her eyes.

'I missed you so much.'

Helen opened her eyes and could see from a crack in the curtains that was letting in the first light of dawn that Peter was sitting on the end of the bed. His face was turned away from her.

'I was only gone for eight days.'

'I mean before that.'

'I don't understand.'

'I knew you wouldn't.'

'Now I'm confused. How is your head? You don't normally drink. I was worried about you.'

'I don't like wine. I only had it once before. I don't like the taste. Or of beer, either. I knew you wouldn't remember.'

'Remember what?'

'We used to be friends. A long time ago. You said we'd always be friends. I missed you so much.'

'I'm confused.'

'You said we'd always be friends. It was a promise. I knew you wouldn't keep it. It was by the stream. I took so long to find you.'

'Peter, you're scaring me a bit now.'

'We used to walk really far together. One time we found an old factory. It was a long way away and my mum would have been angry if she'd known. Nobody was there, but there were shoes. They were very old. You tried some on. I saw you every day, then you were gone. I didn't get big for a long time and then I did. I looked for a long time before I found you. I came here and I watched for a while. I wanted to make sure it was you.'

'OK, Peter, I need you to leave now.'

He stood and she was once again reminded of his baffling, incongruous height. She remained frozen beneath the covers while he walked across the room. As he opened the door to the landing, light streamed in from the big curtainless sash window out there, illuminating his face, and she could see tears on it.

'I just wanted to know you were OK,' he said.

She did not move until she'd heard the front door click shut. About a minute after that, she permitted herself a glance through the curtains. About a hundred yards away, through a light morning mist that the sun was already eviscerating, she could see him making his way to the end of the street, hands deep in his sleeves, then turn and open the driver's door of the dark blue Japanese off-road vehicle.

'I'm done,' said Donna Rooney. 'Knobheads, needy freaks, players, liars, stalkers, big babies, the lot of them.'

'Except the good ones,' said Alice, through a cough. 'But they're usually hiding something.'

The two of them and Helen were in a café on the east side of the city. Three weekends earlier, Mark had dropped the bombshell that over the last six months he had been having an affair with a mature Spanish student of his, with whom he would imminently be moving into a flat in London. This had prompted Helen to reconnect with Donna, but largely as a listener. Helen had said little about Peter to Donna or her mum. As they knew it, she had simply got briefly involved with 'a weird guy', who had seemed OK at first but had become a bit too obsessive. It was entertaining to hear the two of them rant about the opposite sex, becoming a double act of sorts, after which – contradicting much of what she'd just said – Donna departed for a pub on the east side of the city, where she was due to meet her date for the evening.

Helen and Alice continued along the river, in no rush to get anywhere in particular. When they reached the university and the crowds thickened, the volume of people appeared to tire Alice out. Helen noticed how much smaller she appeared here, so much less indomitable than on those cliffs near her house. Human character was more subject to geography than was generally acknowledged. Yet there was a pressure to be the same person people had come to expect everywhere you went. It was one of the small, untold difficulties of life.

The summer had got sluggish and dusty around the

edges. Helen continued to feel very present in her life, largely avoided the noise of the internet, but meditated nowhere near as much as she intended to. She justified this by deciding that she was in a residual state of mindfulness, carried over from the class in spring. She tidied the garden and told herself that was meditation, since, as she'd been told, there was no right way to meditate. It was about making your own rules. To further suppress a more general feeling of untidiness in the air, she'd finally got around to properly organising the spare room a couple of weeks ago, in anticipation of Alice's stay. In a drawer stuffed with receipts, she'd found a piece of lined A5 and unfolded it to reveal the note from Rob, the man who'd come to the museum, who she now remembered as two kind eyes poking out of some coarse dark hair. In an impulsive but philosophical mood, hugely aware that two months can be a very long time, she called the number on the piece of paper, and the two of them arranged to meet. They got on effortlessly, and met again. She was surprised to discover that underneath all that beard he was six years younger than her, often speaking eagerly about concepts and experiences she'd been through and out the other side of, with a naivety that was at once charming and a little irritating. In other ways he appeared older than he was. He knew a lot about fossils and followed *The Archers* obsessively. He co-ran a homeless shelter. He confessed that on the worst days it made him want to walk through his front door at night and collapse on his flat's cold floorboards.

Helen continued to be mildly stimulated by her job and the night classes and cinemas and drinking holes of the city, but she had recently begun to feel something drawing her away from it, in the direction from which she had once come – just a little tug on a sleeve at first, then more. It was heightened by five days in Alice's company. She saw sky in Alice's eyes, a different kind of weather in her cheeks. In her dreams, Helen continued to visit the rope swing on the tree, and the stepping stones. She no longer cut her head on branches as she swung. Other images that came to her made her wake feeling even more sure she was revisiting a version of the countryside surrounding that first house that she, Alice and her dad had lived in. The recesses of a steep space between cliffs. Trees growing almost perpendicular to the mulchy ground. The house higher up the slope and the well behind it. She would often emerge from the dreams feeling a very strong sense that someone had been holding her hand. In one dream she saw Peter waiting for her behind an old stile that had been chewed to a smooth curved edge by horses. Some of the footpaths were streams.

It all made her want to take advantage of Alice's visit by asking her more about the house. Alice said she mostly just remembered it as very dark, small windows. A dingy hollowed-out slice of land, where it rained significantly more than it did even a mile away. She loved the north coast of Cornwall, but not that house. Helen knew that had been the place where Alice and her dad had broken up and she was aware that it was tainted by that for Alice, so she didn't press her for too many details.

'Did I have any friends there?'

Alice took a drag on her roll-up. 'No, and I always felt bad about that. It was another reason I was glad to move. But you were a very self-sufficient child. You always found ways to amuse yourself. I let you wander for miles on your own. Well, not miles, but far. People probably wouldn't do it now or they'd think I was a bad mother. Maybe I shouldn't have done it, but I always had a strange confidence in you to come back safely.'

Helen delayed introducing Rob to Alice for a long time, not because of any uncertainty she felt about him, or their future as a couple, but because of the weight of similar introductions from the past, and the anxieties and disappointments attached to them. She needn't have worried. When she and Rob finally ventured west together the following January, it was less reminiscent of the uneasy encounters between boyfriends and her mum in the past and more reminiscent of the times in her teens when platonic male friends had come over to the house and hit it off instantly with Alice: Jason McMaster from next door, maybe, or Warren Stafford, whose band she'd played a bit of violin for. That was not to say there was anything platonic about Helen and Rob's relationship. She still felt a pleasant cube of warmth open up in her chest in the moments before she saw him, even if she had only last seen him a few hours previously. There was no terror in the excitement that went with discovering each other because the excitement soon began to feel underpinned by a realisation that when it faded, it would be replaced by something else, something different, but no less rewarding.

Some parts of him, she was sure, would never stop amazing her. One was his astonishing lack of geographical savvy. He was a man who, faced with a choice of three footpaths, could be guaranteed to choose the one that made no logical sense. A non-driver from a landlocked town, he sat in the passenger seat looking as guileless as a plump, recently birthed woodland creature while Helen negotiated the last few miles to Alice's beneath inverted waves of black metal rain. 'So that's the sea over there, right?' he asked, pointing to the countryside to the left of the road, entirely overlooking the elevated horizon to the right, with its rim of cracking light, which to Helen's mind in every way possible screamed, 'Ocean!'

He put his trust in her totally, like a child, on the three long walks they took that week: only one of them in the additional company of Alice, who was struggling with a trapped sciatic nerve. Unassisted, it was a little tricky for Helen to navigate the two of them to the old house between the steep cliffs, especially since she ambitiously chose not to go the road way, and the footpaths here, a mile or two inland from the coast path, were little trodden and barely marked at all. They scrambled down a near-vertical bank of copper-green ground, finding it impossible not to break into a half-run, and emerged at the end of a lane with grass up the middle.

Helen recognised the first house immediately: the old knobbly walled place that had been empty back then but, while still knobbly, now had the neat look of a holiday cottage. Clean linen curtains, a front garden of trimmed cordylines and sharp-edged beds. Alice and Helen's old place, sixty yards further down the hill, was less welcoming. Dark brick stained darker by weather. Grouting equipment piled on a small window ledge. Piles of broken propagation trays on a wet and untidy winter lawn. The sweet sound of running water filled the air and in her mind's eye Helen could pinpoint where the stepping stones were but, disappointingly, they were not visible. They could smell a faint bark perfume from the woodyard a quarter of a mile further down the hill, where the village properly began. As a whole the area was smaller than in Helen's dim memories, which she'd anticipated, but it was also less accessible, more hemmed in by dead foliage. There was no public access to the stepping stones and, even when Helen climbed the wall, she could not quite see them. The well, meanwhile, was only a rumour.

Alice was right: it was an unusually dark area. On top of the hill behind the cliffs, the sun had been having a ding-dong battle with the clouds, coming back to set a cold sparkle on rooftops and damp walls every time it looked like it had been defeated. But here it couldn't break through. The ravine had been carved out by nature in such a way that there was a barrier on all sides. Helen now, for the first time, had a sense of how difficult that final winter, after her dad left, must have been for Alice, in a dark place like this, in a house that let in minimal natural light, looking after a child alone, with an only intermittently functioning car. But in the rush of memory that the place provoked in Helen, loneliness was not the central characteristic. She did not recall it as a sad place. Just as the foliage was blocking her route to the terrain where she'd done most of her playing as a child, her memories were frustratingly out of reach. She had new recollections: two ponies a little further down the hill where the light came in and there were always oxeye daisies in summer, a no-longer-existent village post office where every morning her mum collected a newspaper with her name on it from a small pile. A jellyfish sting. Spotty images. The wood smells helped nudge her mind into the past, but they weren't enough to take away the blotted edges of any mental photos she possessed.

'I've only just fully realised what a bumpkin you are,' said Rob. 'Can we have a pint? I'm gasping.'

After thirty-six years, Helen was still finding more out about Alice. Rob's presence was perhaps a factor in that. It was as if Alice suddenly had two children, which gave her double the reason to reveal information they might not have known about her. He helped her get an old music centre out the loft and a few dozen LPs. The three of them drank two and a half bottles of wine and Alice and Rob danced to 'Strange Brew' and 'The White Room' by Cream. Alice told them what a huge part of her life dancing had been before Helen was born, how her dad had stifled it, the revelation she'd felt when she did it again, twenty years later, at a salsa class in Bude – all new facts to Helen. Helen found out exactly why Alice had quit her teaching job in Launceston. The caretaker had been making suggestive comments to some of the female teachers, being particularly relentless with Alice's friend Christy Noll, and once cornering her in the store cupboard. Alice had finally lost patience and reported this to the headmaster, who had shrugged it off, offering the opinion that it was a sad situation when a man was judged for expressing his appreciation of a woman with honest words. 'He was a hideous dickbag,' said Alice.

When Helen was out at Sainsbury's, Alice told Rob about the time Alice had got lost in Cheltenham on the way to meet her friend to see a band, then spotted a man carrying a flute case across a square in the town, who offered to walk her to the venue, since he was going there too. It was only later that Alice realised he'd been the lead singer of the band who were playing. Their name was Jethro Tull. 'Why has she never told me that?' Helen said to Rob, offended.

By March, Helen and Rob had made the 360-mile trip west again to do some gardening for Alice, who was now struggling a lot with her leg. It was the beginning of another alternative new year and Helen recognised herself only in segments from thirteen months ago. She'd always been a quietly self-assured person, but her sense of self was different now from what it had been then, reflected back at her solidly by a few people who knew her, rather than flimsily by a lot of people who didn't.

The dreams about the house in the dark valley continued: not every night, and not every dream featured Peter, but some did, or some simulacrum of a Peterish figure. Once, walking past the Sweetland Meditation And Yoga Centre, tipsy on wine, she came within a whisker of mentioning him to Rob, but decided no good could possibly come of it. In June, on an events-management training course paid for by work, she recognised a large-haired, serene woman as Andrea from the meditation course, and the two of them ate lunch together in a small courtyard where blackbirds flitted. Andrea said she'd not really kept in touch with anyone from the course and asked Helen if she had, and Helen said no.

'What about the quiet guy you used to talk to? Paul?' asked Andrea.

'Peter.'

'Yes, that's the one.'

'I don't know. We did hang out for a bit. He sort of vanished. I was actually wondering if you might know what happened to him.'

'No. I think you were the only one he ever really spoke to.'

Helen did not think of herself as self-obsessed or dominant in conversation but, remembering the few weeks she had known Peter, she found herself questioning this. She was amazed at how little she had known about him. They had never become friends on a social networking website; she only knew that he'd lived on the 'east side of the city' and worked 'with wood'. Now the fright of what he had said to her that night at her house had faded, what was left over was an unusual and confusing low-lying guilt. After her encounter with Andrea, the guilt made itself more apparent. She went on Facebook and scanned the friend lists of groups and people affiliated to Sweetland. She tried Peter's number, but it was out of service, as she'd predicted it would be.

One day she took a detour on the way to Rob's, going via Sweetland. At reception, she announced that she was trying to find the contact details for a man she'd met on a course there, because she had some important personal news she needed to get to him. The lady on the desk – another leaflike person with excellent posture – explained that she shouldn't really do this sort of thing, but, perhaps seeing something trustworthy, or marginally desperate, or both in Helen's face, retrieved a red-spined A4 book from a drawer and flicked through it until she found the appropriate section.

'You say you don't know his surname?' she said. 'We have a Peter Brook listed here, from that course. Would that have been him?'

'I guess it must. I don't think there was another Peter on the course.'

'Oh, that's weird: we don't have any address listed for him. But we do have a mobile phone number.'

She wrote down the number for Helen, who thanked her, then, out on the street, checked and discovered with no surprise that it was the disconnected one she already had. Schoolchildren were out, giddy with the imminence of summer term's end. Rob had texted. He was already at Helen's, cooking. He asked if she could stop on the way back and get salad and a bottle of wine.

Alice died in October. It wasn't a recurrence of the cancer, and Helen would be able to look at the situation philosophically one day because of that, but not for a long time. Alice had done something she tried to avoid at all costs, due to the problems with her eyes: driven at night. She'd been heading back from her friend Marie Reyes's place along the Atlantic Highway and had swerved to avoid a car overtaking from the opposite direction, skidded, and slammed into a tree. It was all very instant, the police assured Helen.

At the funeral Helen was reminded of her mum's immense popularity: her curious combination of solitude and sociability. People poured in, many more than Helen had anticipated. Gardeners, café owners, farmers, artists. The rough stone of the church was stained in a particular dark, large way, which made it appear more matter-of-fact about death's harsh realities than most churches. Outside, the late afternoon was just a long road made of winter. Rob made six different types of pasty. Only he and Helen ate the vegetarian ones, but people asked if he was a professional chef.

After the recent pull she'd felt in a westerly direction, accumulating slowly with each passing month, it was odd to abruptly realise there was no longer anything here for her. Or was it that simple? That was a vast question, and she was far too tired right now for even small questions. She summoned from a small locked compartment inside of her the strength to write to her dad, at the last address she'd had for him. There was no reply.

Helen and Rob took some time off work and went to Cuba for a fortnight. When they returned, Helen had the house valued. She was surprised at the results. You wouldn't call it pleasantly surprised, as there was nothing pleasant about it, but she was surprised. Rob said he'd give it a fresh coat of paint. She said she'd seen the paintwork in his kitchen and he should stick to doing great stuff with butternut squash. For the next three months, she did nothing. The house sat there, the bedcovers still unchanged from Alice's last night in them, a couple of small fragments of moss on the pillow, mementoes of her final day on earth as a gardener. A hole in the conservatory roof reopened in a storm. A couple of young walkers with imaginations leaning to the macabre saw the place from the footpath at the back, became intrigued, looked in the window and spotted a dead mouse and a dead crow on the floor, beneath the hole. On their way back out of the garden they glanced at the garden table and noticed that on top of it was a pygmy-shrew skull that Alice had found on the coast path the previous year. Six miles later, in the pub in the village where Alice and Helen used to live, the walkers told each other stories about the house and decided that somebody, either recently or less recently, had been murdered in it. Then the monthly folk music session started in the pub and there were other subjects, more immediate, to remark upon. When the female walker, who wore a red anorak, went to the bar, a drunk old man ran his hand down her back and made a remark, and they decided to leave.

When Helen herself thought about the house, she felt sure nobody had ever died in it, or that, if they had, it had at least not been in tragic circumstances. She had always slept well in it, despite the noise of the weather up on that high point behind the cliffs. It had been full of Alice's positivity and clutter: her art, her car-boot trinkets, her attractive rugs. It wasn't until Helen had actually booked an estate agent to take the photos that she asked Rob if they could have a chat. There weren't as many jobs over there, not in the fields that the two of them were trained in, but there were some. She had seen a few in events management. And he had been saying for ages that he wanted a change. The cooking. Why not? They could get by, for a while, until they worked it all out.

It wasn't easy at first. They had their first proper arguments, ones that lasted a day or two. She, a born bumpkin, fell guilty of a classic city-to-country relocation misconception: that she'd be taking the easy, relaxed elements of one kind of life and adding them to another set of easy, relaxed elements, rather than replacing one with another. Shopping – especially with one car that they shared, now Rob had passed his driving test – took planning. It rained every day for a fortnight and the lane flooded, making it impossible to get out and into town. The conservatory became a small enclosed lake when the hole in the roof reopened.

Rob seemed at more of a loose end than her, and he rattled against her nerves. 'What are you doing?' he would ask, when the answer, invariably, was that she was doing exactly what she'd been doing the last time he'd asked her, twenty minutes earlier. She wondered if she'd made a mistake, if the isolation would break them. But when he got a job in the kitchen at a café in Holsworthy – not quite the adventurous position he'd been looking for, but with a nice enough boss, and flexible part-time hours – it began to get easier.

Helen never felt bored here. When she was not working on the house or applying for jobs, she found herself writing about Alice, trying to remember details about her life, for fear some might slip away. She wrote with the speed and freedom of someone writing only for themselves. The house was slowly becoming hers and Rob's, but there was still so much to go through. In a drawer of bills and old lists in Alice's workroom she found receipts that showed that Alice had been selling her embroideries of the Cornish landscape to local galleries. Rob spoke to the café, and they agreed to have an exhibition of her remaining work.

In the loft, in a box containing Helen's old schoolwork and drawings, she found four diaries dating from when they'd lived in the dark house: not hers. Alice's. The entries were sporadic, often with infuriating gaps of over a month between them, sometimes with references to names with no explanation of who they were and sometimes very mundane, but Helen was transfixed. The voice startled her with its innocence, its uncertainty, and she at times found it hard to equate it with the image of a sixty-something Alice on the clifftop, charging up and down steep paths, shrugging off life's injustices or laughing throatily into the rain at something scandalous. The very early entries offered little clue into what life had been like with her dad, but those from their last six months at the dark house were more expansive and chatty.

3 March, 1984

Walked down into the village with Helen today. Bought milk, eggs, couldn't find garlic anywhere. Don't think it's reached Cornwall yet.

17 March, 1984

A wet day. Nothing good on the radio. I think I would like to escape this place and live in Athens, or Sicily. I want to climb hills in stifling heat and get skin like an old handbag and not care. I want to be free, but I don't know what that means right now.

20 April, 1984

Helen said she has been playing with the boy from up the hill again. I don't know what boy she means and there isn't one up the hill, because nobody has lived in the house for two years, since

Florence died. I suppose her family will sell it, eventually. Helen is such a bright child, it would not be a surprise if she had an imaginary friend. I will ask around. I think she walks quite far on her own, so it could be a boy from the village. She said they play Pooh sticks.

Helen's breath caught. To her it felt sharp, almost like a shout, and she was surprised to find Rob still asleep beside her, the heat of his breath on her forearm. It was as if she assumed that he knew her so well that the turmoil in her mind would have woken him. She read the last entry again. Then she read on.

3 May, 1984

We sat on the clifftop at sunset tonight and it was beautiful. A night like this makes me want to paint the whole world. Found some lovely fabric at the market in Wadebridge on Saturday. I think I will make a dress from it.

7 May, 1984

John is ill. I will try to visit him tomorrow, and bring some shopping. Must get food for Henry too. Probably just offcuts from butcher.

9 May, 1984

For a friend who is imaginary – that is, if he is imaginary – Helen's boy pal is very detailed. She said he is tall and has dark hair and that he is nicer than the boys at school, who always tease her. She said when he grows up he is going to be ever so tall – taller than her dad, or Mr Watkinson at the post office. She brought back a stick, which had a sharp, whittled end. She said he whittled it for her and his name is Peter. I took it off her and told her it's too sharp to play with. I also told her that she mustn't go near the well, but she said she doesn't anyway, because Peter doesn't like it. 'How long have you known him?' I asked her. 'For always,' she said. 'But he wouldn't let me talk to him when I was too little.'

17 May, 1984

Brown water coming out of the taps again. Apparently about a third of the village has it, not just us. Helen nagging me to read to her again. Always wanting more. I like it too, it's such a pleasure to have a daughter who is so enthusiastic about stories and learning, but I could barely keep my eyes open.

18 May, 1984

Helen came in with the bottom of her dress ruined. She said she and Peter had crawled through a hole that led to a stone where King Arthur's sword is and that he killed a dragon, and that Peter has a sword of his own, which is just as good. I think she has some of her information garbled. Must get her a pair of new trousers. Also need my shoes reheeling. Down to just one pair now, as others got ruined in the mud. Car needs MOT this week. It all comes at once.

21 May, 1984

Derek our postman must be at least sixty, probably older, but he still has an entirely full head of hair. I doubt he has lost one strand. We want to congratulate men when we see this, but why? It's not like it involved any special effort on their part.

29 May, 1984

I am bored. Today I did something I have never done before: I went into the village pub. I didn't even want a drink. I recognised a couple of faces in there, nobody by name. Everyone looked around as I walked in. A whoosh of air. I thought that only happened in stories and films. Bob the landlord knew my name, and where I lived. It's not surprising: if you're a single mother in a village this size, you don't get away with anonymity. He seemed nice enough. 'You're next to the old Arnold place, aren't you?' I said I was, and talked about what a lovely kind lady Florence had been. He said he'd heard the family were selling it too, and he hoped that whoever moved in didn't get put off by the history. I asked him what history. He said the drowning. I asked him what drowning. He said the boy who'd fallen in the well. It was a long time ago now. Back in the early fifties. The dad made tables. The woodyard had been his, once. Personally, that kind of thing wouldn't bother him, when buying a house, but he knew it put some people off.

8 July, 1984

I don't want to be here any more. It is so dark. It's July, for God's sake! Where is the light? I am keeping Helen in more (I say that like she is a dog). She is fidgety and upset.

* * *

After this, there was a four-month gap, and no more references to the dark house. Alice talked about her new teaching job, her garden, recipes, Helen's first few days at her new school in Launceston. Her tone was different, less frustrated. Helen read each of the previous nine entries again, then again, then again. Each time, she felt that if she read hard enough, she might find some new clarification, an extra detail.

She got up and went to the bathroom, had a piss, brushed her teeth. A grey streak had emerged over the last six months, in her fringe. Rob said it made him fancy her even more and had given her a new nickname as a result: the Sex Badger. She did not dislike the nickname as much as she pretended to. She remembered she'd left the heating on, went downstairs to turn it off. The curtains were open and the vast night stared back in at her. It took a while to grow accustomed to the sounds a house made at night and she was almost there.

A shift was taking place. There was stuff you couldn't hold on to that you hoped you might. Friends from the other side of the country were falling away, not always intentionally. Life was rearranging its furniture and settling into a new rhythm. By the anniversary of Alice's death, Helen had settled into a new role, working for a charitable arts foundation, based at a country house. It was a longish, worthwhile commute. Rob was retraining under a fairly well-known chef: an author, formerly the presenter of a now nearly forgotten TV show. They saw each other less, planned their time more carefully. After taking flowers to Alice, Helen thought about the unrealistic ways that death is packaged. Beneath the graves you could see in the churchyard, there were countless others, long forgotten: so many that it had changed the actual height of the ground. People bought into the unscientific idea that the troubled souls came back in spirit, and when they did, those people then expressed a scientific-seeming certainty that these souls were always frozen in the age they were at the time of death. Who wasn't troubled? Or maybe there was a line between A Bit Troubled, and Truly Troubled? Who decided where it fell? Who adjudicated crowd control in the afterlife? There was a notice in the church foyer about bat conservation, explaining to people that bats were not actually evil. Who had originally decided that bats were on the side of the bad guys? Where was the hard evidence?

The route from the church to home went past the site of Alice's crash. Helen had not been able to drive that bit of road for over six months, and had sought out alternative routes, but now she took the direct route. Seven loose hens pecked about at the crossroads, near an old stone cross, on the site of an older stone cross. She slowed to a crawl as she turned into the drive, remembering the deep rut at the start of it and the increasingly brittle state of her car. Rob was out. He was always out, nowadays.

The house's walls were thick, but when she was inside, the growing wind of the evening felt like it was in there with her. She lit a fire and tried to hurry the flames along with Alice's old bellows. She drew the blinds in the conservatory at the rear of the house, but always kept the curtains open on the other side, which looked out on to the mile of fields before the ocean. At the point where the first field ended there was a line of young trees. From this distance, in the final moments of dusk, they looked like thin nervous men, uncertain about adulthood, but if you went out to check you would discover that they were definitely just trees.

FOLK TALES OF THE TWENTY-THIRD CENTURY

OLD KING IDIOT AND HIS GOOSE

It had been aeons since the country had experienced a genuine simpleton as its sovereign, so when Old King Idiot took over, he was a great talking point among the population. 'Old King Idiot/Old King Idiot/Got a goose in his bed and a chapatti on his head,' went the popular playground rhyme of the time, stemming from the rumour that Old King Idiot wore a variety of Indian breads as hats. 'There goes Old King Idiot and his goose,' the royal staff would chuckle to themselves, as Old King Idiot was seen strolling through the elaborate palace gardens, talking to his goose who, for some reason known only to him, he referred to alternately as 'Colin' and 'Anna-Marie'.

Old King Idiot might have been the official ruler of the country, but he was rarely trusted with anything important, and mostly just stayed at home while his cousins went about the real business of overseeing state affairs and fighting wars. His ascension to the throne was generally thought of as an unfortunate accident, due to three of his siblings perishing – along with two thirds of the rest of England – in the second and most devastating of the Red Plagues. For the monarchy, it could be best viewed as a temporary blip, and it was just a matter of getting by as best they could. After all, Old King Idiot was very old and would die soon, as would his goose, who now had a noticeable limp. But little known to his family and the general public, Old King Idiot was not an idiot at all; he was an extremely shrewd and learned man: the most shrewd and learned, in fact, that the monarchy had seen at its helm for centuries. His outward asininity was just a facade to enable him to avoid all the royal duties he would have hated, such as posing for media photo shoots and opening malls. While his brothers and sisters and cousins did bullshit stuff like that, he had time to read books and hang around with his transgender goose, who was also brighter than any of the king's relatives. It was a very nice life. Nice, that is, until the dawn of the Great War with America, when the life of everyone on the island – including King Idiot himself – became irrevocably threatened.

For two years the war raged, and it seemed that the

United Kingdom would have to surrender, finally becoming America's fifty-first state, after so many brave decades of resistance. As the USA's great robot longboats encroached on the shore of Cornwall, the king's family gathered for an emergency meeting in the palace's Great Hall, but it seemed all was lost. Then, from a dark corner, an old croaky voice piped up. It was Old King Idiot.

'Might I make a suggestion?' he said.

'Shut up, Old King Idiot,' said Zirius, the most arrogant and square-jawed of the king's fourteen arrogant, square-jawed cousins. 'Nobody wants to hear from you. Go and play with your goose.'

'No,' said his slightly kinder niece, Delawney. 'Let him speak. It will probably be just some surreal nonsense about leavened bread as usual, but we've tried everything here, so how can it hurt? Let's see what the old crazy prat has to say.'

What Old King Idiot said next amazed everyone. His words were precise, clear and erudite: the result of years of quiet learning, done well away from the spotlight. King Idiot read widely, and, having exhausted much of the rest of the library in the catacombs below the palace, he had over the last few years boned up extensively on robot warfare, and learned the codes needed to crack it. With his knowledge, the United Kingdom's cyborg seal army was able to use the correct binary to thwart the American robot longboats. The nation was saved and went on to live many prosperous years under Old King Idiot, who died at the grand old age of 141, just one day after Colin/Anna-Marie. So was coined the popular saying 'Never underestimate Old King Idiot, or his goose', which is still used to this day in a wide variety of metaphoric scenarios.

BIG LEV AND THE ORIGIN OF
'UNLUCKY THIRTEEN'

It was long into the time of the Self-Righteous Men, and England was divided: not by north and south, as it once had been, but by west and east. In the east, electricity remained, for the moment, and the greedy and dynastically entitled lived well, as they always had, but more so. In the rewilded west, weeds and trees burst through tarmac, and vigilantes roamed back and forth across the wood border, picking off rich travellers with the organic arrows from their organic crossbows, then taking back their spoils to large forest communes and distributing them under the eyes of fox and badger effigies. With the new hunting laws, any man pledging allegiance to Commander Michael under the eyes of God was permitted to hunt any creature, anywhere in England.

One day, a party of seven young, wealthy graduates set off beyond the border to the Moorlands, scoffing at the dangers they had been warned about, as naive men who have never known suffering or hardship are wont to do. 'We will stay in this wild land until we have caught thirteen brown hares,' announced their leader, Godfrey. He had heard the legend of Big Lev, the giant hare who roamed the high moor, but had dismissed it as hokum put about by the pagans and tree fuckers of the New West. And, just as he expected, the first few days of the expedition went smoothly. The pagan highwaymen they had been warned about were nowhere to be seen. As for Big Lev, in their minds he was clearly nothing more than a fable straight from the overactive imaginations of the useless poor. After two days, a dozen hares had been neatly shot and roasted, Godfrey and his party posing with their carcasses and taking images of themselves using the magic boxes on sticks that were still prevalent in the east to send back to their wives and elders. He knew his father, Godfrey Senior III, would be proud of him.

On the third day, the weather altered violently and quickly, as it often can on the Moorlands. Sleet and hail rat-a-tatted on the anorak hoods of the hunters so fiercely that they could not hear each other speak. A wind from the icy security gates of North Hell growled down over the high stones on the moor and screamed pisswords at the hunters' chattering teeth.

'Can we go now?' asked Othelbert, the shortest and least entitled member of the party, as they struggled to set up their motorhomes following a fruitless third day. 'What's the difference between twelve and thirteen hares, anyway?'

Godfrey turned on him with eyes of smarmy purple fire. 'I set out to slaughter and cook thirteen hares, and, by Christ's Chin, thirteen is the number of hares I will slaughter and cook!'

Another day of devil's weather followed, with scant prey in sight. Even the one creature at which Godfrey got a clean shot, an adder, slithered away effortlessly into a hole. Coming over the brow of one of the Moorlands' highest points, Hangman's Tor, on exhausted horses, the men were surprised by a very sharp and sudden incline, and barrelled and zigzagged down it, horses slipping in the fresh mud. Riders and horses hurtled and skidded down the hill, some men holding on for dear life, some dislodged to roll on the peaty ground, clipped and clouted by rocks on their descent. When they finally came to rest, they found they were surrounded by several witches in dark green gowns: exactly as many, in fact, as they numbered men. The witches were gathered around a cauldron, which, in the maelstrom, had been turned on its side. Dark green juice bubbled out of it, onto the tight mossy ground.

'I'm sorry,' said Othelbert, pathetically. 'We didn't mean to.'

'It was foretold, and you have arrived exactly on time,' replied the head witch, although she was really just the witch who was best at public speaking, rather than the head witch in any official capacity, since the witches tended to think of themselves as a democracy.

'We really are very sorry,' said Othelbert.

'It was foretold, and you have arrived exactly on time,' repeated the witch with the great public-speaking skills.

'Don't apologise,' said Godfrey. 'They're the ones who should be apologising to us. Look at them, wretched hags.'

But Othelbert was not listening to him, and neither were the rest of Godfrey's men; they were too busy watching a giant, long-eared form materialise from the green steam where the upturned cauldron lay, becoming clearer and clearer, more brown, and more towering.

'Hi everyone! How you doing?' asked Big Lev, as he became corporeal. 'I'm Big Lev!' And with that, he bit each of the hunters' heads off, spat them out, and turned them into stones.

You can still see the giant stones now if you are travelling the north moor. If you look closely, you will notice that the fine cracks that time has wrought on each stone resemble faces. Their expressions have been said to sum up 'the exact moment where smugness turns into excruciating agony'.

THE MINSTREL AND THE MAGIC SNOW

Once, long before the Great Dark Era that ruptured civilisation, there was a young, awkward man who liked to play his banjo. He played his banjo everywhere he could: at home, high on wild forsaken hills, and in less reputable local taverns. His family encouraged his banjo playing, but none of them could tell him the truth, which was that it sucked in a fairly major way. They knew the man could never work in a conventional office or retail job, as he was too dreamy and impractical, so they figured that at least it was a way of keeping him from the traditional nefarious pursuits of the idle young. He seemed happy, which most people on the border between youth and adulthood weren't, what with the vain and troubling excesses of the electrical era. But with age often comes self-awareness, and one day, when playing his banjo to a raven on his favourite coastal path, and watching the raven fly away in apparent discomfort, an epiphany hit the man.

'Oh woe,' he said to himself. 'I am not the musician I think I am. I am a deluded, untalented fool and I am never going to earn a living playing my banjo.'

Then, curling up in a ball, right there in the middle of the path, he began to rock and weep in a gentle way. The sound he made was not particularly loud but it was nonetheless pathetic to hear, coming from a youth legally old enough to drink mead and ride a tractor, and even the gulls on the cliffs nearby seemed to cringe.

The man rocked and wept in a ball for seven days and seven nights. When he opened his eyes, he looked above him, and there, surprisingly, was the raven that had flown away in fright earlier. It was perched on the arm of a very old, looming man, with a long white beard and a cape. The young banjo player couldn't help also noticing that the clifftops were covered in snow, which was odd, since snow never settled in this region, due to the salty air and mild, damp climate.

'I heard you playing your banjo last week,' said the old man with the long white beard. 'It wasn't the kind of music I personally enjoy, to be honest, but I heard some potential there. Also, you fit into what we're looking for right now.'

'Who's "we"?' asked the young, awkward man.

'Don't you worry about that. Just take this,' said the old man with the long white beard, handing the banjo player a pouch of gold and a polythene bag containing some leaves.

'Oh, thank you,' said the banjo player. 'What's this green stuff in the bag?'

'It's a magic plant. Eat some of it, and it will help you play more colourfully and interestingly.'

'What about all this snow? Where did that come from?'

'That's magic snow, not real snow. But it's not magic in the same way the magic plant is magic. You must never, on any account, lick it or sniff it.'

'Why would I want to lick or sniff snow?'

'I don't know. But just don't, OK?'

The young banjo player and the old bearded man with the raven went their separate ways: the banjo player back along the path towards the village, and the old bearded man through a cavity down into a cave below the cliff edge, which looked for all the world like a shimmering psychedelic portal to a silvery netherworld. The young man's family were glad to see him back, although it had been a busy week for them, what with it being lambing time, and if they were being frank, it had been only in the last quarter of an hour or so that they'd noticed he was gone. That night he plucked his banjo with renewed enthusiasm and, after a couple of tumblers of mead, decided to ingest some of the magic plant the old man had given him. Very soon, a remarkable change occurred: he began to play his banjo more beautifully and colourfully than ever before. It felt almost as if he wasn't actually playing it himself, that the tunes were somewhere in the ether above him, and he was simply reaching up and gently grabbing them, as if they were perfect, docile butterflies.

Over the next few years, the man played his banjo at alehouses and taverns all around the country, drawing larger and larger crowds. Rarely was there a night when a comely young lass did not accompany him to bed and let him ejaculate on or at least around her. Back in his home village, few old friends recognised him as the ungainly lad they'd once called 'Banjo Boy'. His large, awkward jug ears were now covered by a lush mane of hair that made the maidens of the high street swoon every time he walked down it. One even asked him to sign her cleavage, which left ample room for all of his four names. It was only afterwards that he realised this was Eleanor, the girl who'd once planted a cruelly exciting sarcastic kiss on his lips in the final year of school, purely to distract him while her brother crept up from behind and pinned a note to his back, on which was written an unkind phrase.

It was generally thought that the man's first, second, third and fourth albums were among the greatest that had ever been recorded with just a banjo. But, upon recording his fifth banjo-only album, he experienced a bewildering creative block. His magic plant supply – which oddly, perhaps as an intrinsic part of its magic, never seemed to diminish – was not having its usual effect on his songwriting. Taking twice his usual dose seemed, if anything, to exacerbate the hindrance. He possessed so much he'd once dreamed about: his own horse and wagon, seventeen pigs, five banjos, a beautiful girlfriend – plus another, three villages away, in case he got bored – but he felt engulfed by an intangible emptiness.

In desperation, he wandered to that same clifftop path where he had liked to play his banjo as a youth but, not feeling any more positive, curled into a ball again and, as the snow began to lightly fall and settle, started to weep just as he had all those years ago. This time, though, he didn't carry on for seven days and seven nights, since that is a long time to curl up in a ball and weep, and as you get older you develop an awareness of the sanctity of time, even if you're in a jaded period, as the banjo player was. Also, as he sank to the ground, a snowflake landed on his nose and dripped slowly down into his mouth.

'Mmm. That's kind of nice,' he thought, tasting the snowflake. Cupping his hands, he scooped up more of the snow, and began to put it in his mouth and nose.

Then a funny thing happened: the self-doubt he'd been experiencing so acutely recently began to evaporate. Picking up his banjo, he began to pluck furiously, and sing, and the results were phenomenal. Soon he was thrashing around the clifftop furiously, plucking out song after song and frantically stuffing snow into each of his orifices. 'This could be my best work ever!' he said aloud to the big white sky, after laying down what felt like another sweet track. 'I will call the album that will emerge from these sessions . . . *Snow Jesus*!'

Just before the banjo player headed back from the clifftops to the village, he thought he caught sight of a vision from his past, about fifty yards away, through the snow. If he was not mistaken, it was the old man he had met here all those years ago, his beard even longer than ever, the same raven obediently perched on his bare, mottled arm. It was hard to tell, as the snow was falling heavily, and because he really was quite off his face by now, but before the old man turned back to pass through his shimmering psychedelic portal, he seemed to shake his head in a sad way and mouth a sentence which, though indistinct in the noise of the weather, would have been made out by expert lip readers as, 'Same thing happens every fucking time.'

After that, and before his moneyed, lonely death in a beach house thirty years later, the banjo player made five more million-selling albums, each steadily more awful than its predecessor, apart from maybe the last one, which some people called 'a return to form' but mostly in a wishful way that was entirely down to context.

OLD MOTHER KILDERKIN

Deep in the Lincolnshire Fens – a region of the country so unnervingly flat it was said that on a clear day you could see a dog walking towards you from two whole miles away – there lived a youth who worked as a disc jockey. He told people, 'I work as a disc jockey,' but what he really did was just play records all day in his bedroom at deafening volume, if you overlook that one time his friend had got him a gig at a chain bar, to which, after thirty-one weeks, he'd still not been invited back.

Next door to the youth – who was actually twenty-five, and not really a youth at all any more – lived a tiny old lady with nine cats. 'I wondered if you might turn the music down a little, please,' the tiny old lady would ask the youth, but he'd never listen. Sometimes, he'd even turn up his favourite song of the time in response, which was usually extremely bass-heavy with greatly monotonous lyrics. 'Get lost, you old biddy!' he would shout through the wall. This went on for well over a year until one day the little old lady was suffering from a terrible headache and, driven almost insane by the beats coming from next door and the resultant shaking of her furniture, decided to write a gently worded note and put it through the disc jockey's door. This was too much for the intolerant disc jockey, who'd managed to go a quarter-century not having the inconvenience of having to try to see life through anybody else's eyes.

Having read the note, he stormed to the old lady's door. 'Balls to you!' he shouted, as she opened it, storming straight into her living room, as she could not afford a house with a hall. 'You don't know how it makes me feel when the music pulsates through me. You don't know anything. You don't know about people, or life! You're just a shrivelled old crone whose only friends are cats.'

This was his final mistake, since he had no idea he was talking to Old Mother Kilderkin, who had the strength of forty men and had lived for a thousand years, since before the Fens were drained and were populated only by swamp people. With one casual upward slice of her hand, she broke his neck, then, calmly switching the radio on just in time for her favourite gardening programme, proceeded to cut off his genitals and feed them to her cats in a pie.

LITTLE GOTH TWAT

The popular dandy was on an adrenaline high from a comedy show and, all around him, attractive members of the opposite sex fanned and jostled, telling him how much they liked his hair and trousers and jokes. Despite being self-deprecating about his allegedly calamitous love life during the show itself, he did his usual thing of getting his minders to hand out raffle tickets to offer four not quite randomly selected women under the age of twenty-two the chance to have sex with him. But one callow maiden stood out above all the others. Her name was Clematis and she came from a small mining village over the way. Her mother had died from eating pebbles when she was not more than the age Clematis was now, leaving her father to raise Clematis and her brother alone on the paltry wages of a fast-food restaurant employee.

'Ooh yeah, I like you,' said the popular dandy, evaluating Clematis' porcelain skin and bob of meadow-soft hair.

'You can come and live in me big gothic mansion with me in the Southlands. All you have to do is promise to make me trousers for me. As you know, I do like me trousers, ooh.'

Clematis was a very bright girl, but she was also yet to reach that age that women reach when they become more perceptive about when men are being dickheads. Also, the mining village was very hard to get out of, in a social or financial sense, for those searching for a better life, and, with the popular dandy's trousers being such a legendary part of his image, she felt honoured to be given the chance to be directly associated with them. So she accepted his offer and set off to live with the popular dandy in his vast gothic mansion in the Southlands, departing by velvet-lined coach, with her father and brother tearfully in the background, waving their handkerchiefs – which were not actually handkerchiefs but single, recycled kitchen towels, as they couldn't afford real handkerchiefs.

Quite quickly, it became clear that life with the popular dandy would not quite be as Clematis had pictured. The main problem was that, every day, he locked her in a room in the turret of his mansion and would not let her out until she had sewn him a pair of his famous trousers. He was also very hard to please.

'Ooh, these are not me trousers,' he would say, after Clematis had spent a long day sewing. 'They don't have me signature look, guv'nor.'

His demands became more and more taxing: first four pairs of trousers a week, then five, then seven. One day, having stabbed herself in the cheek with her sewing needle through sheer exhaustion, Clematis broke down and began to cry.

'Oh, why did I agree to this?' she said out loud to nobody. 'I miss Father and the village and Jack, and even the old industrial chimney that used to belch black smoke into the air all around.'

Just then she heard a strange low knocking at the door. Opening it and expecting it to be the popular dandy, asking for yet more trousers, she was amazed to see the oddest little thing she'd ever laid eyes on: not more than two feet high, coal black in appearance, covered in cobwebs, and with a long tail flapping on the floor behind it.

'Who are you?' she asked.

'I'm Little Goth Twat,' said the thing.

'That's not a very nice name.'

'No, I know. It's what him downstairs calls me. I hate it. He bought me from a circus a long time ago and promised me a better life, but it was a lie. One of his rich Satanist friends put a spell on me, which keeps me locked in this place for eternity. He gets me out and makes me dance for his guests sometimes. It's no kind of life, even for a stunted otherworldly being. I can't even remember what I used to be called. It was so long ago.'

'He's a bit of a bastard really, isn't he?'

'Yep.' The little thing handed her a handkerchief – an actual one, not a sheet of recycled kitchen towel – which he seemed to produce from a pocket: a curious turn of events, as he wasn't wearing clothes. 'I am sorry you have fallen foul of him too. I would like to help you, though.'

'And how do you propose to do that?'

'I'm very good at sewing trousers, and very quick too. I will take over your job.'

'Goodness! Really? And what will be your payment for this?'

'I will give you three attempts to guess my name. If, by the third attempt, you have not guessed correctly, you must take my hand in marriage.'

'But you just told me your name. It's Little Goth Twat.'

'Oh, for God's sake. I always do that. I'm such a scatterbrain.'

And, without further ado, just as he had done with her eleven predecessors, Little Goth Twat led Clematis down the secret escape tunnel, and opened up the great iron door at the end of it, allowing her to run to freedom.

That night, having finally reached the end of his tether, Little Goth Twat crept into the popular dandy's chamber and used a tiny hammer to cave in his oppressor's skull. This also had the effect of breaking the spell cast by the rich Satanists. As he walked to freedom, he felt no remorse, and wondered why he hadn't done the same thing years ago.

STEVE WHO WAS JUST A TOMATO

Penny cared about the world and what people had done to it. She knew she couldn't save it, but she didn't see that as any reason to stop trying. She was always the last at the farm and spent hours removing small shards of plastic from the compost heap, long after everyone had gone home. Tomatoes and lettuce were her favourites, and she handled them with no less tenderness than if she was handling one of her own offspring, carefully pricking them out by their fragile cotyledon leaves, sniffing them and letting their aroma overpower her. She was good at what she did, but she also loved the mystery of her craft: you could never quite tell what would or wouldn't thrive. In the polytunnel, one particular tomato plant shot ahead of the others, reaching for the stars up the taut baler twine that Penny had lovingly knotted a couple of weeks earlier. What was going on deep underground that made one plant give up a dazzling crop but another barely get out of the ground? Penny liked to attempt to answer this question, trying out a variety of self-made comfrey and nettle feeds and organic mulches, but her inability to ever do so comprehensively was also the driving force behind her love of growing.

It was a calm, sunny afternoon in early June – not too hot, but definitely not cold – when birdsong sweetened the air. Penny had just returned from the post office, where she had been collecting a courier delivery of a parasitic wasp, which she was hoping would destroy the aphids that were attacking some of the tomatoes on the east side of the polytunnel. Law dictated that you had to tell the person at the post-office counter precisely what it was in your package when you were paying for registered delivery, and it made Penny laugh to think of the private seller of the parasitic wasp answering this question with the statement: 'A wasp.' She was still chuckling to herself about this as she bent over to do some watering and was surprised to hear a deep male voice behind her.

'You have lovely hair.'

Penny spun around to see where the voice had come

from, assuming that perhaps one of the people staying on the campsite near the farm had wandered into the polytunnel out of curiosity. It happened sometimes, and Penny was always polite and garrulous when it did. But as she stood upright and looked around, there was nobody to be seen. Questioning the solidity of her own mind, she continued watering the plants.

'I'm sorry if that sounds creepy. I mean it in a sincere way. It has a very natural look. What do you use on it? I'm guessing it's some kind of seaweed mixture. Not that I'd know much about that kind of thing, being almost totally bald!'

Penny shot bolt upright again. She wondered if the person talking to her was hiding, which, even though nothing he had said to her was actually creepy, made it kind of creepy.

'I'm over here. At the back. Keep walking.'

Penny followed the voice until she arrived at her prize beefsteak tomato plant, the one that, while still juvenile and unripe, already seemed in danger of ripping through the polytunnel roof.

'Up here. Look above your head.'

What Penny saw next belied everything she had learned as a student of horticulture. Looking down on her from the top of her most impressive tomato vine was a grinning red face topped with an umbilical cord of green hair.

'I know. It's odd. I don't know how it happened, either. I have decided to call myself Steve. It seems as good a name for a tomato as any, and I'm not really a fan of the more clever names.'

Over the next few weeks, Penny and Steve slipped into an easy routine on the balmy summer evenings when nobody else on the farm was around: Penny watering and feeding the plants and Steve commenting on the way he saw the world, which was in amazing detail, for a tomato. What was nice is that they could sometimes be silent in each other's company too, and it was never uncomfortable. Steve was always showering Penny with compliments: not just about her hair, but about her clothes, her dexterity, and her tolerance.

'It was so exemplary how you handled that,' he said, after watching one of the other growers – a hypochondriac called Fran, whose only two topics of conversation were herself and those who had wronged her – babble at Penny for half an hour. 'She tends to bludgeon people with conversation. You were patient, and nice, but you also showed her up as the idiot she is.'

Sometimes Steve opened up to Penny about some of his fears and hopes. He said he had no idea what he was here for, no idea why he'd been made different from the other tomatoes. It was very frightening sometimes, but he tried not to think about it, and to just get on, stay in the present, and enjoy what was turning out to be a brilliant summer. One evening, when Penny was away, listening to a Bulgarian folk band in a field, vandals rode motorbikes over some of the vegetables: many carrots and butternut squash perished. Steve had shouted, but the vandals couldn't hear him above the engines of their bikes. He used all his strength to bend back his vine, and try to reach a rock lying loose in the corner of the polytunnel, then catapult it through the polytunnel door at one of the riders, but it was no good: he couldn't get there.

'The important thing is that the intention was there,' Penny told him the next day after she'd cleared up and heard Steve's story. 'You might not be a hero, but you're a hero of intention. And that's good enough for me.'

It had been an unusually wonderful summer on the farm, but it still had the natural, seasonal components of all summers, including harvest time, and around eight weeks after Penny and Steve first met, the inevitable pivotal moment arrived. Steve was looking really fantastic by now: big and shiny and succulent. He was in his prime, but he wouldn't be for ever. What should they do? Certainly Steve could live a bit longer, but he would soon decline and be a less happy tomato. And he would be dead and rotting into some compost by winter anyway. It was upsetting, but he admitted it would be better to call it quits now and offer some happiness to others in the process. Penny was relieved that he saw it this way because that was her view on the matter too, and she was in charge. In the end, he was her tomato. As they said their final goodbyes and she tenderly picked him, she thought she saw a kind of peace descend over his features, but maybe that was just what she told herself to make herself feel better.

Steve was served as part of a village barbecue the following week to raise money for refugees. He was stuffed with shallots, Parmesan, fresh sage and parsley, halved, and shared by a cashier from the village shop and a man who designed solar panels. The cashier believed her half was a little smaller but chose not to vocalise this opinion. Steve tasted amazing but, ultimately, not markedly different from any of the other tomatoes on offer that afternoon.

SEANCE

Sssshhh. I can hear something. Has anyone left a washing machine on in another part of the house? No. OK then. Yes. This is something. I am sure of it. The veil is wavering. It has become granular and I can see through it but I am not using my eyes. Sssshhh. Can you feel it? Keep your hands on the table.

He says his name is Ian, and he was a cyclist. OK. Yes. It is coming through now. He died in a car accident. I talk to a lot of entities from the other side and what I have learned is that when you die suddenly, and become a ghost, you are not at first aware that you have passed over. You carry on what you were doing just before the incident that caused your death. This was the case with Ian. As his body lay inert in a field in Devon, where it had been flipped by a speeding oil delivery driver, who now continued towards Newton Abbot under the impression he had merely annihilated one of the West Country's larger deer, Spirit Ian continued to cycle happily up the lower hills of Dartmoor. 'Morning!' he called to a middle-aged couple with a labradoodle, cheerfully, as he cycled past Whiddon Scrubs. They ignored him. 'Shitbags,' he said under his breath. Ian is telling me all of this now. He talks quickly and has a lot to say for himself. He has had nobody to chat with for a while and is very lonely.

Ian felt unburdened as his mountain bike propelled him up towards the top of the moor, and looked back with satisfaction at the contours he had covered so far: it reminded him of a giant green version of his duvet at home, after the twins had bounced on it, in that way they often did when they woke him and Judith up in the morning. Judith had made him a brie and cranberry sandwich for his ride but he didn't feel hungry, which was strange since all he had eaten so far today were nine prawn crackers from last night's Chinese: slightly stale and rubbery, the way he preferred them. He felt like he never needed to eat again. The cycling was effortless, too. He is telling me all this now. His voice sounds like chalk, in a comforting way. It is a helpful voice, full of concessions. He thought he'd take advantage of the effortless feeling by taking the longer of the two routes he favoured, which went up past the reservoir and to the place where they said fur-covered hands reached out of the mist and pulled drivers off the road, although Ian had never seen any himself. He stopped every mile or so to admire the sky, which was full of small densely packed clouds but contained rectangles of bright light that shone down into the arable fields at the moor's edges, as if God was playing a joke on particular sheep and cattle by announcing that they were the Chosen Ones. Ian had noticed a cyclist pressing along the lanes in his wake, at first maybe 700 yards behind him, then closer. The cyclist was dressed all in black, to match his bike, and wore a hat, not a helmet. As the cyclist closed in, Ian noticed that his bike was very old: not a bike anyone sensible would choose to negotiate rugged landscape like this, if any reasonable budget was available to them. On the next plateau, Ian waited for a band of insouciant wild ponies to cross the lane, and decided to let the other cyclist catch up and pass him, because the cyclist's presence was starting to feel quite claustrophobic, inasmuch as you can ever feel claustrophobic in a national park area measuring 368 square miles. It had now been seven hours since Ian had eaten or consumed any liquid and he still did not feel hungry or thirsty. He also had not thought about sex for nearly as long, which was possibly the longest he had gone without thinking about sex since he was twelve. Ian is telling me this now, all of it. Still talking quickly. As the other cyclist got closer, he noticed that he was male and wore very dirty clothes. His hat was made of felt and had moss and lichen stuck to it, which made Ian suspect that before the other cyclist had reached these lanes he had taken a very overgrown route to the top of the moor, possibly cycling across heavily tussocked ground, fraught with peat bogs.

''Ere mate, get the hell off my patch. I've been here since 1962,' said the other cyclist. Ian noticed that the spokes on his tiny pathetic black bike were also coated in a spider's web of lichen, plus several actual spider's webs.

'I'm sorry, I was under the impression it was a free country,' said Ian.

'Well, you were under the wrong impression. Since when was anything in this country free? What's free about this: you work all your life for Mr Wallace, and you finally get your promotion, and you celebrate by going for a picnic, then a Triumph Spitfire spins off the road, and crushes your skull beneath its wheels.'

'I – I don't understand.'

'Oh, bloody Nora. You haven't realised yet, have you? You're dead. We're both dead.'

'What?'

'Have you not noticed some big differences? Has anybody spoken to you recently? Have you had an appetite? No? That's because you're no longer living. You are of the planet, but no longer on it.'

'But why are we both cycling?' Now Ian looked at the man again, he noticed that his complexion was not like the complexion of most people he came across in everyday life. His skin had a dark look to it, a touch of dust. But it did not look like the skin of a dead person, just like skin from another time, far away. Further away than 1962.

'When you're dead, you do the thing that made you most happy, forever. Cycling up here made me happiest when I was alive. You'd think that was OK, but it's a different story, when you're stuck doing that thing for all of eternity. I've been up here for over half a century now. Try doing that, and still getting a thrill from having the wind in your hair. Anyway, I'm not here to stand around and chat. And I'll be blowed if I'm going to put up with a young nitwit muscling in on my manor.'

'So, what is your manor?'

'All of it. The whole moor. So, bugger off and find your own place. Try Somerset. It's very flat in places, and has some lovely gorges, but bear in mind that they sometimes make it with their cousins.' With that, the black rider aimed a kick at Ian's mountain bike, knocking it to the floor.

Ian is telling me this happened a fortnight ago. Since then he has been searching for a place where he could be a ghost cyclist, to no avail. He says that on his way down from the moor he in fact crossed paths with two other spectral presences, including the floating form of a hanged woman buried at a crossroads on unconsecrated ground, but he was still so upset at the revelation about his own death, and the way the black rider had spoken to him, it didn't really faze him. He says he has a question for us. The question is, 'What are some dependably quiet cycle paths on the South West Peninsula?' He says he has an important message too, which . . . Oh. Damn. He's dropped the connection. Don't worry. That happens sometimes. He may return later.

Oh, OK, OK! Listen. Sssshhh. Keep your hands on the table. Something else is coming through. A woman called Adrianna. She is short, dressed in black and orange. Oh, it is becoming clear now. Adrianna is a wasp! She was reincarnated as one, but didn't realise at first. It only dawned on her when she noticed how much time she was spending hanging around bottle banks, and how all her previous logic seemed to have left her when it came to finding the easiest way to get out of houses and rooms. But Adrianna doesn't want to talk about that. She wants to talk about her previous existence, as a life coach. She says that despite being a life coach she also had a life coach of her own, which, when she told people about it, made them mistrust her own expertise as a life coach. She wants to talk about some of the skills she picked up, when redecorating houses, and trying to make them neutral to increase their sales potential. Actually, Adrianna is quite boring. Do you mind if we don't talk to her, and I drop the connection?

I just want to add at this point that I do offer an additional service, which is crystal evaluation. But there is no pressure. For those who don't know what crystal evaluation is, here is an example: in Weymouth last week I dangled a crystal over a man's testicles and detected a shadow there. It might not have been anything significant, possibly benign. The man questioned how I could possibly know there was a shadow on one of his testicles, and chose not to believe me, but the shadow was there. I can guarantee you of that. It will make itself known at some point. As I said, though, there is no pressure. I also write. My debut novel has been acclaimed by some significant luminaries, although I am yet to find a publisher. For those of you who might have contacts in that area, it is something you might keep in mind.

'IHAVESEENTHROUGHTHETUNNELOF LIGHTTOTHEGOLDENTREEOFWISDOM ANDBATHEDINITSRICHSAP.'

I'm sorry I have no idea what that was. Sometimes I just get tremors and snatches, nonspecific voices, I don't know where they're coming from. Some are very vociferous. They can leave me feeling spent for days. Like an electric toothbrush whose battery light is flickering, asking to be recharged. Oh, this is interesting. SSSSHHH. I am feeling fur. Quite coarse, not particularly pleasurable to stroke. It's a fox. A vixen. I believe she was shot near Kibworth in Leicestershire in 1938. The night smelt of vegetables and a dry innocence, an implication of coal. She had been on her way back to the den with two thirds of a pigeon. Before that, she was another fox, and another fox, and before that two previous foxes, bigger, who were in fact distantly related. Essentially she has just been a long succession of foxes over the course of several centuries, and now she is the ghost of a fox, so she can't speak. She has no words to offer us as gifts for our path. But I know she wishes us all well. She wants us to succeed, and remember that life is about the present, and valuing the little things, those apparently insignificant moments that can surprise you and stick with you and make a memory. Yes, animals come through the veil. They're as likely to as people. More so, even. History has lasted a long time and it has contained many, many animals. Pardon? Really? Oh, OK, I am sorry if that is disappointing, or if you feel you have been misled. Yes, I do take on board that you were hoping for some family members. I was too. A revered grandfather or significant tortured aunt. I am afraid that hasn't happened today. Another day it might. The fact is, this stuff isn't on tap. You can't control it. Yes, I can leave. Our allotted time is nearly up anyway. I need to be in Budleigh Salterton by eight. I would prefer it now, in cash, but we can discuss all that later, if you prefer. Well, perhaps. I personally think that's deeply unfair, but we all have a right to our own opinion. Yes, I would, right now, very gladly, but I believe somebody has blocked me in at the end of the driveway. True, but I'm not comfortable with tight manoeuvres, and it's quite new. At this stage I don't quite trust myself. To be absolutely frank, it's only a lease. If you just edge back two or three feet, I'll fold my wing mirror in, and I should be fine.

AN ORAL HISTORY OF MARGARET AND THE VILLAGE BY MATTHEW AND FIVE OTHERS

We were down Tractor's house an his mum and dad was out, so he got these razmags out from under t'settee to show us, an they were pretty rough, dint do nothing for me, but Rocker an Wayne were going 'Phwoar' an that an saying that this woman who were nude an in this barn seeing to these two blokes who were both on bonk looked like Mrs Lewis from Maths, but she dint at all, an even if she did, I dint know why you'd want to look at her doin that. For a bit I were worried that Wayne an Tractor was going to get their nobs out an I started lookin at these trophies that Tractor's dad had for fishin even though I dint gee a toss about t'trophies but then Tractor an Wayne got bored an we went out in back field to ay a kick-about. I went in goal, which I were shit at, but Tractor an Wayne were always trying to do this scissor kick like that bloke who played for Mexico did in t'World Cup. Wayne would flick t'ball up then Tractor would do t'scissor kick, even doin t'commentary that t'bloke on telly had done when t'Mexican guy had done it, but it never looked like it did on telly. I dint give much of a fuck about footie anyroad, I just had a pretty good ball, which were same make as t'one they'd used in the World Cup, which made everyone talk to me more at school, even though when they did I always got put in goal.

About t'fuckin trillionth time Tractor done t'scissor kick, he got it way out an t'ball went over the crossbar. We dint have a crossbar, or even posts, just my bag and Tractor's coat to mark them out, but everyone knew where t'crossbar were anyroad an it definitely went over it, an when it did it kept on going an landed in Old Red Eyes' garden, which were five doors away from mine an me mum's. We called her Old Red Eyes but she only had one red eye, but she were about fucking eighty an everyone were right scared of her. Her lip were all messed up too. Her lawn were all overgrown an one time when we were doing t'Grand National over t'fences down Potash Lane Wayne said he stopped in her garden an looked in her shed an she had about twenty footballs in there which, 'cause it was Wayne talking, means if he was telling t'truth there was probably about seven in there. Sean from up t'road said he went in there too an looked in her back window an there were all these stuffed animals there, squirrels an all sorts, even this massive fuck-off badger an a hare which were just as big, and when he was looking at it her face just appeared at t'window, not saying anything, just gormin at him with her eyes: the red one an the one that was sort of normal.

'Go an get t'ball, Jammo,' goes Tractor.

'Gerrit yersen!' I goes. He could wank himsen off backwards an swivel if he thought I were going in there.

'Mardarse,' goes Wayne. 'It's your ball anyway. Your fuckin loss, yoth.'

Stanley Clarke (vicar): 'What a lot of people don't remember is that until quite recently, the village still had a pinfold. I say "until quite recently"; I mean until some time in the late forties. Of course, it wasn't in much use by then, but there was still the odd animal which would escape and be brought there until its owner collected it – sometimes a cow, or a pig, or even just a pet dog. I remember one of the Critchley children, Margaret, had been very good at bringing back the animals when they got loose. She even brought old Wilcock's horse back there one time. This tiny girl, pulling a huge cob up the hill by its bridle. It was quite a sight! She did have a way with the animals, Margaret, even at that age.'

We went down t'rope swing over Miner's Brook after that, then walked up back to church by Babbington

Woods an Tractor dared us to put us hands on t'electric fence. Wayne wunt do it an Tractor called him a mardy bastard, but I did it an it dint hurt as much as I thought, but felt fuckin weird, like a whole cricket ball goin right up my arm. Sean were in t'churchyard when we got there, sitting on t'bench with this girl Lisa who kept comin up here from Il'son, wi' his hand down t'back of her jeans.

'All right, Patty? Ay, did you hear Cary Grant died?' goes Sean. He called us Patty 'cause I'd once got the bus all the way into Notts just to get a Jamaican patty from the market in the Vic Centre, then come straight home. Everyone said I stank afterwards but I dint an they were dead good patties an I reckoned it were worth hour an a half round trip and 30p bus fare. I'd done it about fifteen times in all but I dint tell anyone else that, after they took piss t'first time. Sean knew I knew Cary Grant were dead. 'Bout a year ago when Cary Grant died, we was all sitting on t'hay bales up in Sean's dad's barn and all of a sudden I remembered that it had happened, an I said, 'Did you all hear Cary Grant died?' but all t'rest had already been talking about it for about twenty minutes an I ant realised 'cause I were off in my own world. I dint hardly even know who Cary Grant was, ant even seen any of his films; I'd just heard it on t'news that morning an said it to try to say summat interesting. Now Sean wunt let me forget about it.

My mum called times like that 'Matthew Moments': these bits of t'day when I'd just go blank an not hear stuff around me, usually because I was telling stories in my head. Scary stories mostly. I were always doing it at school too. The last time I was on bus back from Notts after getting a patty I sat with this girl Sarah who sat near me in History who'd gone into town after school too, but to get a record, not a patty, and she told me that I was weird because I was really dozy but not in a stupid way, like all the remos at school that do classes in the new block. I could have taken it in a good way but I dint think she meant it that way. Then she got the record out and asked me if I'd heard of the band who made it, who were called something about Giants. I said I hadn't. Straight after that, she saw Adele Perry at the back of the bus, who was in History with us too, an went to sit with her instead. I opened my can of Coke an was holding it between my legs to try to be quiet an a bit spurted out an Adele said really loud, 'Look, he's doing a piss!' so all of the bus could hear.

Dorothy Wilcox (miner's widow): 'Folk come here from other parts and think people don't give much away or waste words, and think that's just the local character, that it's just country folk not liking outsiders, but it's more than that, if you ask me. There were stuff that happened here a long time ago and it ant been forgot. Tongues wagged and people got accused and there was consequences. I'm not going to say the word, but you know the one I mean. You can see marks on the houses, between the bricks. The older ones. That history don't just go away, even after centuries, and some of the families what suffered are still here. You won't find me gossiping, though.'

It were always ones who was older, like Sean, who made up nicknames. No bastard calls me Matthew or Matt no more, cept for teachers an me mum. Tractor an other kids at school call me Jammo or Jameson, but most everyone else in t'village calls me Patty now. Sean was t'one who started calling Tractor Tractor too, 'cause once a hay bale fell off t'back of one when Tractor was working at Sean's dad's farm an hit Tractor an Tractor dint even fall over or move much; he just stood there. Sean dint have a nickname himsen, but maybe that were because he dint have any friends who was older than him. My mum said I shunt hang out with him 'cause he was a bad influence, an Mrs Gainsborough at number 13 said she saw him sniffin glue behind t'church.

Anyroad, we all started walkin, up past Stubby End, an Sean's still got his hand down the back of Lisa from Il'son's jeans an Wayne's tellin Sean bout Red Eyes an our ball, an Sean says that she's well fuckin weird an tapped, an that this one time his mum said she saw her out in back field talking to a rabbit like it was her friend, an that this other time she turned up on Sean's mum's doorstep, carrying this box wi' fruit in it, an tried to sell her it, an the fruit was fucking rank, all with grubs comin out of it an shit. Sean calls her Red Eyes too but he says it different to us, I can't do it, the way he does it, but he says it like the Eyes bit is bigger than the rest. He says it a few times as we walk, an Wayne laughs, like just sayin someone's name in a stupid way is funny if Sean does it. It were nearly getting dark now an I thought we might play dobby in t'churchyard, but I don't think Sean wanted to do that 'cause of Lisa. Last time we played dobby, Sean lifted up this board at back of church leading to a cellar an dared me to go down an said there were fresh bodies in there that had just died but I chickened out. Church were right spooky at this time of night but I liked it. A few times I been up there with Tractor an Wayne an Nogger from Awsworth an told them some ghost stories, but I never done it when Sean been around as I know he'd say it was gay. The stories were from this book I got from Il'son library called *Tales for the Midnight Hour*, which had a skull an blood on the front. After I first got it an the night got to t'Midnight Hour I coulnt never sleep 'cause I were thinkin about how that's the time when all the bad stuff happens, but then I thought that I wasn't sure what the Midnight Hour was, if it were the hour that started at midnight or the hour before that, an after that I started going to sleep way better again.

After we was past Stubby End, Sean turns left down in direction of canal an climbs over the fence an says his dad an his uncle are shooting in the field down there an we should go an watch. He takes his hand out from fucking miles inside Lisa's jeans so he can climb the fence but he dunt give her a leg up over it. Fence were quite high an Lisa's legs wasn't, so Tractor stepped in an gave her a hand o'er it. Sean giz Tractor this look then, like a look what'd normally make Tractor go, 'What you fuckin gormin at?' if it weren't Sean who'd gi'n it to him. 'Bout three minutes later we're passing this bit of hedge which is really wet 'cause it rained in t'morning an Sean elbows Tractor into it but Tractor doesn't go right into it an get that wet, he stays pretty solid, like when that hay bale hit him. We can hear gunshots now, coming from t'fields other side of canal.

'I don't want to see them hurt the bunnies,' goes Lisa. 'Sean, can we go an do summat else?'

But Sean says to her not to be such a wet weekend an we cross t'bridge an walk up field an we can see Sean's dad an his uncle now, an Sean tells us to get down, in t'wet grass under t'hedge. I wanted to go back home an read or watch telly 'cause *Back to the Future* were on, but I dint dare 'cause I knew Sean and Wayne would call me gay or posh, like they did when we was playin footie an my mum brought me a sandwich out on thick brown bread with lettuce in it. My mum would be well fucked off if she knew I was here. She hates it when she hears guns an dint even want me to have a toy one when I was little, even though my dad said it was OK. She dunt even really like the village at all an says we only live here because it was affordable an she wanted to be close to my nan an my aunt Jean after she broke up with my dad.

Edward Munnery (schoolmaster): 'I'll probably die here now. I don't see much point in me moving. I'm past the age when I go to another village or another town and I think life will be better there. It will have the same problems or, if it doesn't, it will have others to replace it. This isn't a bad place, in the grand scheme of things, and it has lots of happy memories for me. I still feel proud when I walk past the old schoolhouse, even though they've turned it into the village hall now. I had a good set of kids. Mind you, some could be cruel – as they can in all places, I suppose. I remember that business with the Critchleys – so sad. First the mum, then the dad, all in six months – TB it was – and the oldest girl, Margaret, bringing her sisters and brothers up alone. No social services in those days. The clothes got old and dirty and other children can sniff out that kind of sadness. It's a bit animalistic. A very bright family, though. The others moved away, two to Australia I believe, but Margaret is still here. Well into her sixties now. I don't see her often.'

We could see Sean's dad an uncle now but they coulnt see us. Sean's uncle had three dead rabbits strung over his back an Sean's dad had a sack an that probably had more in. Sean's uncle and dad both look same, like their faces been chiselled out o' stone, but Sean's uncle is taller an looks like t'stone were harder to chisel. Last year one of t'swans on t'canal got shot an it was in the local paper an everything, an Tractor told me it were Sean's uncle that done it an also that he sold Wayne's mum stolen central heating for her house. My mum could only afford one car, an that kept breaking down, but Sean's uncle had two, an a Land Rover too. One time he was driving t'Land Rover down near Notts in Meadows an a bloke's body got shot an fell out a window into back of it. That was in t'local paper too, but everyone knew that Sean's uncle dint shoot the bloke an the police got the bloke who did.

There were some rabbits running about down near where we was sitting an I was worried that Sean's dad an uncle would shoot them, an that if they missed the bullets might hit us 'cause they couldn't see us, but Sean's dad and uncle was pointing at summat down in the far end of field, down near Miner's Brook. I dint want to see a rabbit get shot 'cause I knew if I did I'd probably think about it for yonks afterwards, probably in t'Midnight Hour, knowin me. I was already even thinkin about what it'd be like thinkin about it when I saw this rabbit run through the grass really fast, over where Sean's dad an Sean's uncle were pointing their guns, an then I cottoned that it weren't a rabbit, it were a hare, because they're bigger an way faster. Sean's dad an Sean's uncle both took two shots at it but they missed an it kept weaving from side to side, like it were trying to confuse them, like when Maradona scored the goal against us in the World Cup an he was confusing our defence – not t'goal where he used his hand an cheated, t'other goal. Sean's dad took another shot an missed but then when hare were weaving quite near to where I was sat, Sean's uncle did another shot an it caught the hare on its back leg, on the side nearest me, the left one. It weaved again then, but as it did it slipped a bit, like it had only realised the bullet had hit it quite a while after it had, an it made this fuck-off scary noise that went right through me. But it didn't quite go down, it got back on its feet, an ran off towards the bottom hedge – slower, not all zigzaggy like earlier, but still way faster than a rabbit.

It were really quiet in t'field after that. Sean's dad an Sean's uncle had run off down the ridge after t'hare an when I looked around to the side of me, Sean, Wayne, Lisa and Tractor weren't there any more. Weather had gone really weird, too, like it were trying dead hard to rain again, but couldn't. It felt like when you want to chuck up but there's nowt in your stomach any more an like the sky was a stomach. But I think as well as that an Sean an the others not being there any more why it seemed so quiet was a bit 'cause of that noise that the hare made. I'd heard t'noise rabbits made when they were hurt an I didn't like it, but it weren't like the noise the hare made. I can't do it 'cause, like I told you, I'm rubbish at impressions, but it were kind of like the hare weren't just saying it were hurt, it was like it were explaining why.

Shane Worthington (mechanic and hare enthusiast): 'The lips start to split when they get older, and you see their teeth more. They're only about three when they die. I used to think they lived longer. I don't know why – maybe because they look wise. "Woodcat" me dad used to call them. "There's old woodcat, going home," he'd say, if we saw one in t'field. Did you know they can get pregnant when they are already pregnant? Right freaky, int it? I still don't get how it can happen, even though I've read how. There were a lot more here a few year back. They'd run around together, in threes and fours. If you got near one, it wouldn't always run away, not like a rabbit. Sometimes it'd stay to watch you for a while.'

There didn't seem much point in hangin around after that, specially because if t'sky did finally get around to puking up I dint have me jacket with me. I walked back over t'canal where there was always torn-up bits of razmag in t'reeds an went the way home that went down by Stone End Farm 'cause it were almost proper dark now an that got me to t'road quicker, an Sean's dad an Sean's uncle probably wunt be goin back that way. To tell truth, I weren't thinking about much, just about what me mum might be makin for tea, and I'd forgot about my ball altogether, but when I got to Red Eyes' house I remembered it.

I don't know what made me walk up her path really, but there were no lights on in the house an I just had a feeling when you know somebody isn't there, so I thought I might as well go an get the ball, if it were still there, 'cause me mum had paid quite a bit for it. The house weren't that spooky really; it were just different to the other houses on the street. It didn't have any plastic or white bits, an nobody mowed the grass, but I dint know why people were always on about how important it were to mow grass anyroad. One day when me mum got me to mow ours I saw a black beetle run away from where I was mowing an I started thinking about all t'other insects that probably han't got away from the mower, an all the other lawns in Derbyshire and the world, an all the other insects, being mowed every day, an I couldn't stop thinking about it for yonks. I don't remember ever stopping thinking about it really – it just happened, without me realising, like when you stop hiccuping when you been hiccuping for ages but you can't say exact moment it happened, you just aren't hiccuping any more. There must have been loads of insects in Red Eyes' garden, an they were probably much happier than in Dennis an Rita's next door, where they were always spraying stuff on their lawn an it looked like a golf green.

Joanne Jameson (single mother and post office worker): 'Some people in the village like to stand about and chat, and some don't. I don't think that just because someone is quiet and keeps to themselves it's any reason to think there's anything wrong with them – sometimes the opposite. I know the children say stuff about Miss Critchley because of the way her house looks, and I didn't get to know her well, but she once brought me a basket of delicious fruit. There were sloes, and blackberries, raspberries too, and the most delicious russet apples. I can still taste those apples now and remember biting through the rough skin into the flesh. So pure white and flawless.'

I suppose someone must have cut or mowed some bit of Red Eyes' garden one time, or it would be a massive jungle an not even a garden at all, but it must not've happened since ages before I were born, an that made it harder to find my ball, but it still only took me a coupla minutes.

It were trapped in some brambles behind the greenhouse, which wasn't a greenhouse any more, more of a greyhouse, but I got into t'gap without getting cut an got it, an I was thinking how Sean an Tractor probably wouldn't ave been as brave as I was being, but when I was going down t'jitty between t'hedge an garage I heard a click which sounded like someone going into t'house an I froze totally still. I knew I should have left back way 'cause all it would have meant was that I'd 'ave had to climb back fence then walk along back field an go in the back way to my house, but now if I went back that way I'd be goin right in front of Red Eyes' back window, but if I carried on an walked out front I'd be going right 'bout four foot past the side door, which I think were what had made t'click.

I still thought front way were probably best, so when I'd waited about three minutes an hant heard nothing else, I walked forward, not too quick an not too slow, an all the time keeping my eye on the front gate that were my target. I were tryin to be really determined about it but when I walked past door I coulnt help it, I looked to the side through it, like summat else made me do it. It were open an Red Eyes were sitting just inside it on this chair, cryin, an clutching on to her leg, the left one, holding this bandage on it, an it were bleeding all over the floor. She were looking right at me but it weren't like she were angry, just sad, like she were asking me stuff, but not asking for anything *from* me, an like she'd known I'd been there all along. Listen, right, I'm not bullshitting, but I don't reckon as long as I fuckin live I'll forget that look. I went home then an it were summat about that look that made me not tell me mum anything about it, I mean, it were more of a reason than her bollocking me for going in Red Eyes' garden or going about down near canal with Sean an that lot. We heard t'ambulance about ten minutes later an me mum rushed to the front door but the reason its siren were on were 'cause it were goin, not comin.

Anyroad, this were more than two months ago now. Me an my mum moved in with my nan a bit after that. I know Red Eyes were all right 'cause I heard me mum talking to Dennis an Rita at number 14, which int called number 14 any more 'cause they took the number off the door an changed it to 'Brookview', just before we moved, an they was saying that Margaret had had a fall an had to go to hospital but that she were already 'back on her feet'. Me nan said that about me mum when she were talking to me about us moving into my nan's, too: that it were only for a while, until me mum were 'back on her feet'. But me mum hadn't hurt herself. I'm nearer school now an there int no churchyard nearby an Tractor's been moved into another class in t'new block so I don't see him much, but I still tell scary stories sometimes an some of me mates like 'em. Nights are darker now an it seems to make people want to hear 'em more, like t'other week when I got detention an I told a few when Mr Copley fucked off to do summat or other. Most of them come from that book, to be honest, they're not mine, but I add my own bits sometimes. Sometimes I forget a bit an make a bit up an then the new bit sticks an is still there the next time. But I dint add any bits to this one. It's just how it happened. I dint change one thing.

ACKNOWLEDGEMENTS

Thank you to all the readers who pledged towards this unusual, not very commercial book, believed in it and helped make it exist. Thank you to my mum, Jo, for providing artwork for the inside, and to Joe McLaren for the jacket image, which was inspired by a photograph I took of two sycamore trees on the way down from the top of Kinder Scout in January 2018. Thank you to Jecca and Cathy Light for telling the story that inspired 'Just Good Friends' on a chilly night in Norwich just after Samhain. Thank you to my agent Ed Wilson, my editors Simon Spanton and Imogen Denny, Kate Quarry for copy editing, and the rest of the team at Unbound for all their hard work. Finally, thank you to ghosts, for maybe being real.

A NOTE ON THE AUTHOR

Tom Cox lives in Devon. A one-time music journalist, he is the author of the *Sunday Times* bestselling *The Good, The Bad and The Furry* and the William Hill Sports Book of the Year longlisted *Bring Me the Head of Sergio Garcia*. His most recent book, *21st-Century Yokel,* was longlisted for the Wainwright Prize 2018.

Unbound

Liberating ideas

Unbound is the world's first crowdfunding publisher, established in 2011.

We believe that wonderful things can happen when you clear a path for people who share a passion. That's why we've built a platform that brings together readers and authors to crowdfund books they believe in – and give fresh ideas that don't fit the traditional mould the chance they deserve.

This book is in your hands because readers made it possible. Everyone who pledged their support is listed below. Join them by visiting unbound.com and supporting a book today.

Chris Allen

Judy Allen

Nicola Allen

Kathy Allso

Amanda

Elisabeth Amnegård

Mairead Anderson

Sara Anderson

Tamsin Andrews

Emma Anger

Misha Anker

Stevi Apel

Nancy Apple

Julie Archibald

Sandra Armor

Rick Arneson

Diana Arseneau-Powell and
    Alun Wyburn-Powell

Kay Arthur

Sue Arthur

Dawn Ashford

Julie Ashton

Louise Ashton

Dawn Atherton

Tom Atkinson

Paul Atlas-Saunders

Janna Avon

Terri Babbitt

Duncan Bailey

Lindsey Bailey

Nancy Bailey

Susan Bakalar Wright

Susan Baker

Emma Ball

Phil Ball

Jan Ballantyne

Ali Balmond

Jools Banwell

Nicholas Barber

Rosie Barnett

Samantha Barnett

Jenny Barragan

Sara Barratt

Julian Barrett

Louisa Barrett

Jane Barrett-Danes

Diane Barry

Sue Barry

Sarah Bartlett

Jade Bartolf

Lisa Barton

Katy Barzedor

Paul Basham

Laura Baughman

Leslie Bausback

Gisele Baxter

Pauline Bayfield

Ally Beal

Kristen Beck

Samuel Becker

Robin Beckerman

Callum Beesley

Alison Beezer

Kay Belk

Donna Bell
Mike Bell
Elena Belyakova
Chrissy Benarous
Alison Bendall
Linda Bennett
Pauli Benney
Yvonne Benney Basque
Anita Benson
Rebecca Benson
Sue Bentley
Suzanne Bertolett
Tracie Bettenhausen
Mary Bettuchy
Helen Bevington
Clare Bevins
Karen Beynon
Suchada Bhirombhakdi
Heather Binsch
Maggie Birchall
Chuck B. Bird
Elaine Bishop
Helga Björnsdóttir
Rhian Blackmore
Andrew Blain
Cecilia Blanche
Amy Blaney
Graham Blenkin
John Blythe
Megan Boing
Caroline Bolton
Alice Bondi

Christen Boniface
Alex Booer
Jeannie Borsch
Chloe Botting
Val Boud
Lesley Bourke
Lynn Bourne
Chelsea Bowerman
Judith Bowers
Joth Bowgett
Rowan Bowman
Teresa Bowman
Karen Boxall
Jo Boyne
Elizabeth Bradley
Steve Bradley
Aisha Brady
Hugo Brailsford
Paul Brailsford
Angela Bray
Vanessa Bray
Caroline Bray and Finn
Gemma Bridges
Stacia Briggs
Tom Brimelow
Rhiannon Brislee-Young
Charlotte Broadhead
Marianne Brøndlund Jensen
Rebecca Brook
Aimi Brookes
Jennifer Brown
Karon Brown

Kathleen Brown

Leigh (Grotbags) Brown

Michelle Brown

Richard Brown

Sally Browning

Sian Brumpton

Marie Bryce

Catherine Bryer

Elaine Buckley

Gary Budden

Erica Buist

Helen Bulbeck

Janet Bunker

Rachel Burch

Frank Burge

Peter Burgess

Jane Burkinshaw

Julie Burling

Paul Burman

Joseph Burne

Donna-Marie Burnell

Chris Burns

Christina C Burns

Jane Burns

Jo Burt

Alex Burton-Keeble

Heather Bury

Andrew Buxton

Gemma Byrne

Vivian Cafarella

Judi Calow

Donatella Campbell

Lynn Campbell

Lara Canfield

Toby & Ruth Canham-James

Josh Capewell

Catherine Cargill

Susan Caroline

Caroline Carpenter

Liz Carr

Doree Carrier

Lorrie Carse-Wilen

Jess Carter

James Casserly

Tricia Catford

Susan Catley

Stephanie Cave

Rachel Cawthorne

Caz

NJ Cesar

Justin Cetinich

Kathryn Chabarek

Chris Challis

Nicola Chaloner

Tamasine Chamberlain

Liz Chantler

Patricia Chaplin

Celia Chapman

Samantha Chapman

Zoe Chapman

Claire Chappell

Heather Chappelle

Jane Charlesworth

Ailsa Charlton
Gill Chedgey
Rose Chernick
Gill Child
Charli Chmylowskyj
Fiona Church
Amy Ciclaire
Adrian Clark
Nancy Clark
Rebecca Clark
Heather Clark-Evans
Adie Clarke
Helen Clarke
Mandy Clarke
Katie Clay
Penne Clayton
Gill Clifford
Freyalyn Close-Hainsworth
Jessie Clutton
Suzy Coates
Sandie Coleman
Gina R. Collia
Sally Collins
Paul Colnaghi
Bridget Comeforo
Dom Conlon
Brida Connolly
Trisha Connolly
Susanne Convery
Sarah Lucifer Salem Teufel
    Lestat Conyers-Nolan
Jeff Cook

Judith Cooke
Clare Coombes
Fi Cooper
Sue Corden
Íde Corley
Ellie Cornell
Amanda Corp
Adele Correa
Anne Costigan
Kati Cowen
Jo Cox
Dan Coxon
Ann Crabbe
Melissa Crain
Julie Craine
Sara Crane
Claire Crawford
Charlotte Crerar
Simon Crimp
Cara Crocker
Tessa Crocker
Martin N Crook
Nancy Crosby
Elli Crown
Leah Culver-Whitcomb
Tanya Cumberland
Sarah Cusworth
Victoria D'Arcy
Nicole D'hondt
Beth Dallam
Patricia Daloni
Jackie Daly

Claire Daniells

Fi Darkling

Nick Darlow

Elizabeth Darracott

Claire Davidson

Karen Davidson

Bethany J. Davies

Gill Davies

Lisa Davies

Meryl Davies

Rob Davies

Sandra Davies

Catherine Davis

Donna Davis

Laura Davis

Sandra Davis

Jeannie Davison

Mark Davison

Alexandra Dawe

Rebecca Dawson

Philip de Jersey

Joanne Deacon

Alison Deane

Geraldine Deas

Frances Deaves

Joanne Deeming

Nat Delaney

Jamie Dempster

Lucy Dennison

Abigail Dent

Albert Depetrillo

Laure Deprez

Elly DeVall

Suzie Dewey

Sue Dewhirst

Miranda Dickinson

Claire Dickson

Katrina Dickson

Lisa Dineen

Tracey Dodd

Emma Dolan

Catherine Donald

Susan Donnelly

Sarah Dorman

Marina Dorward

Nicholas Douglass

Anna Dramsheva

Katy Driver

Kathryn Drumm

Stacy Dry

Eileen Ducksbury

Jane Duke

Rebekah Duke

Heather Dunn

Julie Dunne

Lucy Dunphy

Amanda Durbin

Pene Durston

Stacey Earley

Dawn N Earnest

Rachel Easom

Christiane Eck

Sarah Eden

Catherine Edwards

Elizabeth Edwards
Sharon Edwards
Eirlys Edwards-Behi
Nia Edwards-Behi
Maegen Elder
Esther Ellen
Tom Ellett
Jamie Elliott
Ember
Dawn Erb
Raelene Ernst
Jeanette Esau
Pascalle Essers
Ceryl Evans
Karen Evans
Dee Ewing
Rachael Ewing
Joe Fairbairn
Jeffrey Falconer
Gina E. Fann
Alison Faraday
Sarah Farley
Charlotte Featherstone
Michael Feir
Welsh Felix
Emily Fennell
Lori Ferens
Peter Fermoy
Sue Fielding
Suzanne Fielding
Erika Finch
Fiona Finch

Hayley Finch
Vivienne Finch
Anna Fisher
Dave Fisher
Jodie Fletcher
Vicky Flood
Fiona Floyd
Janet Floyd
Theresa Flynn
Sarah Foister
Aurora Fonseca-
   Lloyd
Jack Fontana
Sheena Ford
Beverly Forehand
Irene Forse
Anna Forss
Christine Fosdal
Cat Foster
Edward Foster
Fi Fowkes
Lily Fox
Julie Francis
Philippa Francis
Tiffany Francis
Julian Francis-Lawton
Fay Franklin
Nancy Franklin
Jacki Freeman
Mary Freer
Karen French
Cynthia Friedgen

Jo Friend

Rebecca Frost

Sally Fulham

Steve Fuller

Deborah Fyrth

Sharon Gabriele

Sarah Gaede

Lynn Gale

Majda Gama

Frank Gannon

Saffron Uma Gardenchild

Ian Gardiner

Laura Gardner

Christine Garretson-Persans

Dana Gavin

Sam Gawith

Claire Gibney

Rosalind Gilberthorpe

Andrene Gill

Laura Gill

Gill and Ian

Joanne Gillam

Katie Gillingham

Jessica Gioia

Lisa Gironda

Elizabeth Gladwin

Jayne Globe

Sharon Glosser

Sue Glynn

Georgie Godby

Jennifer Godman

Nick Goff

Caroline Goldsmith

Susan Goodfellow

Helena Goodman

Rachel Goswell

Toby Gould

Helen Goulden

Pat Gower

Donna Gowland

Natalie Graeff

Jayne Graham

Sioned Graham-Cameron

Karen Gram-Skjoldager

Emma Graney

Fiona Gray

Peter Gray

Darrell Green

Hayley Green

Marc Green

Liz Greenlaw

Rebecca Greer

Michelle Gregory

Amy Gregson

Judith Griffith

Amy Griffiths

Cathy Griffiths

Louise Griffiths

Rachel Griffiths

Lisa Grimm

Sharon Grimshaw

Helen Grimster

Claire Grinham

Natasha Grover

Rebecca Groves
Juliana Grundy
Geoffrey Gudgion
Martin Gunnarsson
Laura Gustine
Laura Guy
Sara Habein
Terri Hackler
Carol Hadwen
Janine Hale
Anna Hales
Fay Hallard
Lisa Hallett Howard
Emma Ham
Lauren Hamer
Laura Hamilton
Sharon Hammond
Stephen Hampshire
Margaret Hand
Samantha Handebo
Lizz Hann
Kate Hannaby-Jessop
Thomas Hansell
Cathy Hanson
Emma Harcourt
Lisa Hardi
Emma Hardy
Jan Hargrove
Hilary Harley
Candy Harman
Lynda Harpe
Sue Harper

Joanna Harpur
Rachel Harrington
Danielle Harris
Fran Harrison
E Ruth Harvey
Kay Harvey
Anya Hastwell
Luke Hatton
Marianne Hauger
Christian Haunton
Kate Hawes
Emily Hawkins
Denise Hayward
Kate Haywood
Rebecca Haywood
Elspeth Head
Bethan Healey
Gillian Heaslip
Emma Heasman-Hunt
Katherine Heathcote
Katherine Helps
Lynne Henderson
Heather Henry
Eliza Henshaw
Elizabeth Henwood
Anneka Hess
Diane Heward
Anne Hiatt
Jan Hicks
Laura Higgins
Lesley Hill
Emily Hine

Bendy Hippy
Richard V. Hirst
Beth Hiscock
Elise Histed
Greg Hitchcock
Kahana Ho
Jackie Hobbs
Becky Hodges
Alexandra Kate Hodgson
Alice Hodgson
Jason Holdcroft
Rocki Holder
Zoe Holder
Dianne Holland
Samantha Holland
Fran Hollinrake
Claire Holliss
Kim Holmes
Vanessa Holt
Tigger Hooper 2001-2018
Alan Hooppell
Pamela Hopkins
Sharon Hopkinson
Clare Horne
Antony Horner
Philippa Hornsby
Andy Horton
Kevin Horton
Peter Hoskin
Belinda Hosking
Susan Housley
Jacki Howard

Warrick Howard
Cherie Howe
Elli Howlett
Robin Hubbard
Sally Huggins
Jennifer Hughes
Yvette Huijsman
Daniel Hull
Sandy Humby
Kim Humphries
Marian Hurley
Jessica Hurtgen
Claire Hutchinson
Alison Iliff
Dagny Ingram
Marie Irshad
Robert Iwataki
Ali Jackson
Judith Jackson
Sherridon Jackson
Susi Jackson
Clare Jackson Spark
Lindsey Jackson-Kay
Kellie James
Sandra James
Nickie Jane
Kim Jarvis & Peter Taylor
Jocelyn Jazwiec
Luke Jeffery
Barny Jenkins
Heather Jenkins
Vicky Jenkins

Christine Jenner
Niki Jennings
Lisa and James Jepson
Jo Jex
Tristan John
Chrissy Johns
Alison Johnson
Andrea Johnson
Kitty Johnson
Caroline Johnston
Pauline Johnstone
Kaz Jones
Kelly Jones
Meghan Jones
Myra Jones
Suzi Jones
Alice Jorgensen
Sara Joseph
Melissa Joulwan
Alex Joy
Mary Joy
Denise Joynes
Anne-Marie Willard Jullien
Marc Kalfsbeek
Susan Kassab
Frances Keeton
Claire Kelly
Rebecca Kemp
Aidan Kendrick
Christina Kennedy
Ros Kennedy
Denise Kennefick

Debbie, Graeme, Rigby,
    Charlie & Dudley Kerr
Mary Kersey
Helen Kershaw
Audrey Keszek
Evren Kiefer
Dan Kieran
Stephanie Kilb
Peta Kilbane
Denise Andrea King
Janet T King
Stacey King
Joanne Kinson
Pete Kirkham
Jules Knight
Lisa Knight
Mel Knott
Patricia Knott
Rick Koehler
Laurie Koerber
Sandra Kohls
Daniel Kontos
Christy Kotowski
Helen Kramer
Kraze & Simey
Marlies Krueger
Laurie Kutoroff
Jenni Kylan-Mcleod
Samantha Laabs
Kevin Lack
Susan L. Lacy
Stephanie Lahey

Tara Lambert
Peter Landers
Kristi Langli
Patricia Langner
Alex Langstone
Simon Lankester
Joelle Lardi
Barbara Lavender
Terry Lavender
Stephen Laverick
Caroline Lawless
Andrew Lawrence
Jeffery Lay
Stephanie Lay
Catherine Layne
Kim Le Patourel
Katherine Leaf
Debbie Leafe
Diane Leathley
Capucine Lebreton
Diane Lee
Jay James Lee
Desmond Lee & Carl
    Jukkola
Esther Leeves
Peggy Lefkin
Sam Leivers
Nathan Leonti
Kimberly Lepovsky
Catherine Lester
Marianne Lester-George
Jill Lethbridge

Helen Lewis
Katherine J. Lewis
Marian Lewis
Pam Lewis
Zara Lewis
Alfie & Cobweb Lewis –
    my little angels
Louise Lightfoot
Bonnie Lilienfeld
Jill Lincoln
Susan Lindon-Hall
Diane Lindsay
Steve Little
David Livingston
Vikki Lloyd
Ellen Logstein
Anne Long
Kirrily Long
Madeline Long
Katy Love
Sheila Severs Loveland
Sharon Lovell
Catriona Low
Brigid Lowe
Jennifer Lowe
Snowy Lowther
Rachael Lucas
Helen Luker
Margo MacDonald
Zoe Macdonald
Sophie Macgregor
Kirsteen MacKenzie

Louise Macqueron
Yvonne Maddox
Laura Magnier
Laura Maher
Catherine Makin
Angela Malone
Lynn Mancuso
Claire Mander
Christy Chanslor Mangini
Caroline Mann
Michele Mantynen
Anne Margerison
Charlotte Mark
Sharon Marks
Cate Marquardt
Sue Marshal
Simon Marshall
Wayne Marshall
Lesley Kathryn Martin
Mary Martley
Anna Louise Mason
Catherine Mason
Frances Mason
The Mason-Laurence
    Gallery, Dartington
Suzanne Matrosov-Vruggink
Shannon Matzke
Vicky Maull
Hayley Maye
Mimi Mazy
June McAvoy
Wendie McBurnie

Savage McButtkiss
Yvonne McCombie
Claire McConnell
Megan McCormick
Wendy McCutcheon
Lauren McDaniel
Kathy McDonald-Johnson
Clodagh McElroy
Helen McElwee
Jane McEwan
Tracy McFarlane
Clare Mcglone
Ann McGregor
Allan McKay
Colleen McKenna
Vanessa McLaughlin
Cate Mclaurin
Mandy McLernon
Rufus and Mittens
    McPherson
Erin McSherry
Becky Mcskelly
Denise McSpadden
Erin Melia
Ben Mellor
Stacy Merrick
Nicola Messenger
Erinna Mettler
Emily Meyer
Haley Michael
Elgiva Middleton
Lisa Millar

Eilidh Miller
Ian Miller
Jackie Miller
Scott Millington
Chris Mills
Sara Mills
David Minton
Jacqueline Mitchell
Paul Mitchell
Tina Mitchell
John Mitchinson
Keri Mohror
Sebastian Moitzheim
Rowan Molyneux
Lani Momeyer
Claire Monkhouse
Lucy Montgomery
Kim Moody
Chris Moore
Helen Moore
Kristine Moore
Natalie Moore
Sarah Mooring
Elizabeth Morant
Helen Morecroft
Sharon Morrell
Sandra Morris
Suzie Morris
David Morrison
Katrina Moseley
Stefanie Moser
Rachel Mosses

Julie Mostyn
Sarah Mottershead
Juls Moulden
Philippa Moxon
Sarah Moyle
Florentina Mudshark
Jean Muir
Linda Muller
Sabine Müller
Ryan Mundell
Doreen Munden
Ian Murphy
Richard Murphy
Alison Murray
Claire Murray
Jane, Mollie & Parker
    Murray
Tamara Murray
Meg Murrell-Peloquin
Melissa Mutter
Richard Mynett
Kathy Nagle
Debbie Nairn
Phil Naish & Julie Philipp
Sally Nameche
Victoria Nash
Samantha Nasset
Carlo Navato
Gemma Nelson
Tim Neville
Tamsin Newlove-
    Delgado

Sarah Newton-Scott
Ducky Nguyen
Laura Niall
Valerie Niblett
Nicoilín Nic Liam
Liz Nicolson
Sue Nieland
Andy Nikolas
Christine Nobbs
Kate Noble
Holly Noe
Christy Noll
Hugh Nowlan
Artur Nowrot
Adele Nozedar
Jennifer O'Brien
Luke O'Brien
Su O'Brien
Caoimhe O'Gorman
Mark O'Neill
Siobhán O'Shea
Sarah O'Donnell
Sarah Oates
Sandra Oberbroeckling
Laura Ohara
Kim Olynyk
Deborah Owen
Emily, Jon and Axl Owen
Maria Padley
Earnie Painter
Pam Palmer
Imogen Paradise

Roberta Parigini
Lev Parikian
Richard Parish
Lisa Parker
Rob, Est, Rex and Tabby
    Parker
Samantha Parnell
Soraya Pascoe
Karen Paton
Trish Paton
Gill Patterson
Rob Paul
Beth Pavelka
Sharon Pearson
Erica Pedersen
Janice Pedersen
Karie Penhaligon
Christopher Pennell
Penny Pepper
Manda Pepper Langlinais
Sarah Peters
Caroline Petit
Anthony Pettigrew
Leslie Phelps
Joel Phillips
Lisa Piddington
Kelsey Pilkington
Bethany Pinches
Chad Piranha
Awkward Pisswhiskers
Terri Platas
Hugh Platt

Hannah Platts
Rachel Playforth
Isabel Plaza
Jo Plumridge
Lucy Plunkett
Justin Pollard
Jackie Poole
Kathryn Poole
Patreesha Poole
Jennifer Porrett
Selina Postgate
Becky Potter
Lindsay Powell
Sheila Powell
Laura Price
Sarah Price-Sinclair
Susan E. Priller
Christina Pullman
Lisa Quattromini
Rosie Quattromini
Kate Quayle
Lisa Quigley
Bonita Quittenton
Gosia Raczek
Sue Radford
Helen Rainbow
Lucy Raine
Riana Rakotoarimanana
Laura Ramos
Peter Randall
Susan Randall
Suzy and Chris Randall

Mike Rankin
Tina Rashid
Laura Rathbone
Anne Rawnsley
Angela Rayson
Caroline, Ian, Maggie and
    Padstow Read
Rebecca Read
Julie Rearden
Kerie Receveur
Lynn Reglar
Louise Reid
Susan Reid
Vivienne Reid-Brown
Craig Reilly
Peg Reilly
Steph Renaud
Marie Reyes
Julie Reynolds
Debra Rhodes
Lesley Anne Rhodes
Julie Richards
Lorna Richardson
Fiona Riddell Pearce
Lisa Riffe
Celia Rigby-O'Neill
Meryl Rimmer
Nicola Rimmer
Kerry Rini
Jacqueline Roach
Catherine Roberts
Courtney Roberts

Anna Robertson
Marie Robertson
Matthew Robertson
Louise Robinson
Kathryn & Ian Rochard
    and George Bananacat
Patricia Rockwell
Auriel Roe
Jane Roe
Valerie Roebuck
Stephanie Ann Rogers
Jayne Rookes
Kalina Rose
HJ Rose-Innes
Emma Ross
Catherine Rossi
Vanessa Rouse
Laura Rowan
Matthew Rowell
Roxanne
Sarah Rush
Sam Russell
Claire Ryan
Tori Ryan
Karl Sabino
Teresa Sadler
Sara Sahlin
Katie Sajnog
Ella Jasmine Samuel
Marie Sandland
Callum Saunders
Christine Savage

Sherri Savage
Katie Sawyer
Dorothy Scanlan
Artemis and Leto
    Scantlebury
Julia Schlotel
Jennifer Schmitt
Eric Schneider
Leslie Schweitzer
Anne-Marie Scott
Isla Scott
Sarah Scott
Bill Scott-Kerr
Marie Scoville
Alison Scruton
Jane Seager
Andrew Seaman
Jason Searle
Kathleen Seay
Sian Sellars
Karen Selley
Emma Selwood
Belynda J. Shadoan
Mariese Shallard
Christine Shanks
Lori Shannon
Anna Shannon Ahmed
Geoff Shaw
Iola Shaw
Jenny Shaw
Clare Sherman
Josephine Sherwood

Karen Shipway

Rachel Shirley

Andrew Short

Jo Short

Amy Silvers

Nicola Simpson

James Skeffington

Leilah Skelton

Debbie Slater

Danielle Slye

SmallTeethingBeastie

Carolyn Smith

Charlotte Smith

Christina Smith

Daniel Smith

Gabriella Smith

Hannah Smith

Janine Smith

Kathleen Smith

Lan-Lan Smith

Maggie Smith

Mairéad Smith

Michelle Smith

MTA Smith

Rosemary Smith

Sheila Smith

Wendy Louise Smith

LA Smith-Buxton

Melanie Smith-Langridge

Sharron Smyth-Demmon

Julia Snell

Ingrid Solberg

Soxx Somersham

Anne Sowell

Lyn Speakman

Gem Spear

Maureen Kincaid Speller

Chris Spence

Rosslyn Spokes

Kathy Springer

Debra Spurgeon

Jo Stafferton

Richard Stagg

Janice Staines

Elizabeth Stanley

John Stapleton

Hannah Stark

Rory Steabler

Amanda Stebbings

Ros Stern

Fiona Stevenson

Nic Stevenson

Jason Stewart

Kristi Stewart

Sticky-Sounds Zine

Dawn Stilwell

Beth Stites

Yulanda Stockton

Mary Stoicoiu

Shelagh Stoicoiu

Carmen Stone

Emma Jane Stone

Stephanie Strahan

Duncan Strickland

Jess Stroud

David Stubbins

Rachel Stubbs

Dylan Stump

Amanda Sturt

Nina Stutler

Richard Sulley

Sue Summerill

Helen E Sunderland

Adam Sussman

Laurel Sutton

Helene Swan

Ian Swanwick

Toni Swiffen

Russell Swindle

Kirsty Syder

Angela Sykes

Angie Tanner

Brigid Taylor

Helen Taylor

Katie Taylor

Lesley Taylor

Sarah Taylor

Shereen Taylor

Jennifer Teichmann

Sue Tett

Kim Thain

Sarah Thew

Rachel Thewlis

David Thomas

Pip Thomas

Victoria Thomas

Pierrette Thomet Stott

Claire Thompson

Fern Thompson

Helen Thompson

Mary Ann Thompson

Andrea Thompson, Paddy
and Skippy

Corinne Thomsett

Lynne, Kylie, Donna &
Shelley Thomson

Alastair Thornhill

Donna Tickner

Emma Tilston

Hannah Timkey

Adam Tinworth

Joanne Todd

Delyth Toghill

Stacy Tomaszewski

Crystal Tompkins

Sarah Torr

Costanza Torrebruno

Katherine Torres

Angela Townsend

Awel Trefor

Christopher Trent

Karen Trethewey

Cherie Trounce

Heather Trussell

Kate Tudor

Edie Tuesday

Jac Tunnah

Nicola Turner

Ruth Turner
Sandy Tweedie
Anita Uotinen
Angela Vaites
Lorraine Valestuk
Zach Van Stanley
Anne Vasey
Michaela Verspaget
Richard Vicars
Sally Vince
Vivian Vincek
Paul Vincent
Shelly Vingis
Rosie Vinson
Alice Violett
Kate Viscardi
Jen Vittanuova
Louise Vlach
Leslie Wainger
Allyson Wake
Tim Wakeham
Karen Waldron
Anne Walker
Brooklyn Walker
Mike Walker
Rebecca Walker
Sue Walker
Niki Walkey
Heather Wallace
Lucy Wallace
Keziah Walmsley
Declan Walsh

Joolz Ward
Wendy Ward
Toni Warmuth
Jayne Warren
Ben Warrington
Stephanie Wasek
Laura Watkins
Catherine Watts
Cathrine Watz
Tracey Waudby
Dave Wealleans
Chrystine Weaver
Nina and Roy Weaver
Linda Webb
Susan Webb
M. F. Webb and Sean
    Chitwood
Denise Webber
Selena Webber
Lisa Webster
Ange Weeks
Naomi Weinstein
Chris Weldy
Julie Weller
Christina Wells
Richard Wells
Penny Wenham
Jane Werry
Casey West
Elizabeth West
Fiona Whalley
Sara Wharton

Katy Wheatley
Jane Wheeler
Pam Whetnall
Andy Whibberley
Susan White
Mark Whitehead
Vicki Whitehead
Miranda Whiting
Annalise Whittaker
Helen Wild
Heather Wilde
Peter Wilde
Edward Wilford
Annette Wilkinson
Cherry Wilkinson
Wendy Wilkinson
Lorna Will
Linda Willars
Caroline Williams
Gillian Williams
Hayley Williams
Jenny Williams
Melissa Williams
Rose Williams
Sarah Williams
Laura Willis
Rosamund Willis-Fear
Derek Wilson
Fiona Wilson
Kirsten Wilson

Molly Wilson
Tracey Wilson
Oliver Wilton
Camilla Winlo
Kim Winspear
Caroline Winter
Anna Wittmann
Howard Wix
Gretchen Woelfle
Kanina Wolff
John Wood
Judith Wood
Laura Wood
Rebecca Wood
Laura Woods
Brenda Wordsworth
Emma Workman
David Wrennall
Elizabeth Wright
Melanie Wright
Melissa Wright
Rebecca Wyeth Fox
Jeremiah Wyke
Jo & Luke Wynell-Mayow
Theresa Yanchar
Jo Yeates
Jennifer Yocum
Lisa Zagami
Birgit Zimmermann-Nowak